Like some others before him, Charles combines a life of writing with a career in the insurance business. He admits that his work gives him insights into human nature as exemplified in business dealings, but precious little time for writing.

A Bad Business is therefore his first published full-length novel. In it Charles Deakin has painted several interesting word portraits, especially Malcolm Davidson.

Recommended to lovers of fiction as it used to be written.

A BAD BUSINESS

Charles Deakin

A Bad Business

EMMA
STERN
PUBLISHING

An Emma Stern Publication

Copyright © Charles Deakin 2016

The right of **Charles Deakin** to be identified as author of this work
has been asserted in accordance with sections 77 and 78 of the
Copyright, Designs and Patents Act 1988.

A CIP catalogue record for this title is available from the British Library.

ISBN: 978-1-911224-08-2

This is a work of fiction. Names, characters, places and incidents originate from
the writer's imagination. Any resemblance to actual persons, living or dead, is
purely coincidental.

Published in 2016

Emma Stern Publishing
107 Fleet Street
London
EC4A 2AB

www.emmastern.com
www.facebook.com/emmasternpublishing
Email: editorial@emmastern.com
Email: marketing@emmastern.com

Printed in Great Britain

Chapter I

He looked to be a fit man. That much was clear as soon as he walked through the door.

His features were strong and regular, his face bronzed by exposure to sun and wind. He had cropped fair hair, keen blue eyes, and a firm chin.

Malcolm Davidson had good reason for his confidence. Although barely forty years old, he was nevertheless at the head of a powerful mining corporation. There had been a number of amalgamations, accompanied by power struggles, and Davidson had emerged top of the pile.

He made himself comfortable behind his large desk and buzzed for his visitor to be shown in.

He knew the man, and that explained why he had agreed to see him, although he had no appointment.

'I'm sorry to have kept you, Haynes,' he said.

'I'm used to kicking my heels in outer offices,' Haynes said, and smiled ruefully and sadly.

'Every day Is a busy day in the city.'

His visitor, who had been waiting in an ante-room, and was then esteemed fortunate to be accorded an interview, looked around him with a little smile.

'So you've prospered, Davidson,' he said.

'I always meant to.' Davidson said. He was not a man for small talk or false protestations. 'And you?'

The visitor shook his head. 'I've tried many things,' he said. 'All failures. What is it that keeps some men down while others climb?'

Davidson shrugged. 'If a man's will is strong enough......'

Haynes nodded gloomily. 'Mebbe that's it,' he said. 'I never had the will, or if I had, it didn't seem worth my while to use it.'

'I've a lot on today. Every day, in fact. So I can't give you much time, I'm afraid. Tell me, Haynes. What can I do for you?'

'I want something to do,' Haynes said.

'Meaning?' Davidson said.

'I have to find employment.'

'I doubt I'll be able to help you,' Davidson said, firmly but not unkindly.

'You don't beat about the bush, do you?' Haynes said with a short hard laugh.

'Why should I?' Davidson said. 'It would only waste our time, and be a mistaken kindness.'

'Damn it, Malcolm, there must be something.'

'It's an important business this, Haynes. I daren't risk employing a single weak link.'

'Give me a letter of recommendation to someone else, then,' Haynes begged. 'I'm just back from Africa, skint, completely skint.'

'I can't do that,' Davidson said. 'I know you well. I like you. More than once you have been useful to me........'

'Then -'

'But you were not made for business, or any form of regular work. I wouldn't offer you a place in my own office, and I cannot pass you on to my friends. So - what else can I do for you?'

Haynes laughed bitterly.

'I can lend you some money,' Davidson added shortly.

'I'll take it,' Haynes said; 'but it will be spent pretty soon, and I doubt whether you'll ever get it back. It isn't money I'm after. It isn't even the chance to make a fresh start.'

Davidson shook his head. 'I can't help you,' he said.

'I have to make money,' Haynes said, 'and I need to make it fast.'

The phone rang, and Davidson was busy for several moments answering questions and giving instructions. Then he turned once more to his visitor.

'Haynes,' he said, 'you talk like all the others who come into the city expecting to find it a sort of ....an Eldorado. I can do nothing for you. How much money do you need to get on your feet I don't want to seem unkind, but I'm a busy man. I don't want to lend you fifty bucks today, and have you come and borrow another fifty next week, and another the week after. Ask me for any reasonable sum, and I'll give it. But afterwards we shake hands and part. You understand?'

Haynes leaned forward in his chair. He wet his dry lips nervously with his tongue. The look of ill-health in his features was almost painfully obvious, and so different from Malcolm Davidson's healthy look. There was a paleness that belied the fact he'd just returned from Africa. The writing was clear on his face.

'Look here, Davidson,' he said hoarsely, 'don't think I'm ungrateful. You've put the matter straight to me like a man, and, if need be, I'll ask you for a good round sum and go, and I'll swear on oath you'll never see me again. But listen. I'm in a bad way. I was in the hospital last week, in Jo'burg, and they told me a few things.'

'I'm sorry,' Davidson said. 'Looking at you, it's obvious you're unwell. So why not rest and recuperate? When you're feeling stronger, you can think about finding work.'

Haynes shook his head. 'That isn't it,' he said. 'I'm a sick man. I have been given somewhere about twelve months to live - no more.'

Oh, God!' Davidson said quietly

'I want, somehow or other, before I die, to make a little money. I don't want a fortune - nothing of that sort - but I want to make just a little.'

'You have a wife?' Davidson said quietly.

Haynes shook his head. 'A sister. Kid sister. Poor little bugger, she's wearing herself out working in an office, or something, and I can't bear the thought of leaving her all alone with nothing to fall back on.'

Davidson drummed with his fingers on the table. His manner was not unsympathetic, but betrayed the impatience of a man of affairs discussing an unpractical subject with an unpractical person.

'My dear chap,' he said, 'don't you see that your very illness makes it absurd to imagine that you can take a

10

position and save any amount of money worth mentioning in twelve months? The idea's absurd.'

'I suppose that's what it sounds like, Malcolm,' Haynes said, using the forename he rarely used; where they had been in South Africa, it had always been surnames. 'But listen. You know I have many weak points, but I'm not a coward. I like big risks, and I'm always willing to take them. The quacks give me twelve months - that means, I suppose, about seven months during which time I'll be able to get about, and five months of slow torture in a hospital. I'm not looking for pity. Just the chance to top up my bank account.'

Malcolm Davidson decided that silence was the best response. Let the fellow get things off his chest. He owed him that, at least.

'Isn't there any work you could put me on to where the risk is great - the greater the better - but if I succeed I could make a reasonable sum of money?'

Davidson shook his head. 'My dear chap,' he said, 'we're not in Africa now, you know.'

'I don't mind what I do,' Haynes said.

Davidson shook his head slowly, and then stopped. A sudden change came to his face. He had the air of a man absorbed with an unexpected thought. His lips puckered. A thought had struck him, and Haynes saw it.

'You were always a man to take a chance, weren't you?'

'It added spice to existence.'

Davidson chose his next words with extreme care. He spoke slowly.

'How do you feel......how close do you stand with the law?'

'I've lived a wild life,' Haynes said. 'You too. You didn't get to where you are today, the top, by always being legal, did you?'

'Conscience?' Davidson said, and it was a whisper.

Haynes felt a stirring of excitement.

'My conscience is elastic enough. As much as it needs to be.'

'Is there anything you wouldn't take on?' Davidson said.

'I'd take on anything which means money. You have lots of interests under your control, Malcolm.'

'I have enemies,' Davidson said.

'Be a surprise if you didn't,' Haynes said. 'A man in your position.'

'I need a man with a closed mouth.'

'Silent as the grave,' Haynes said, smiling wanly

'Is it too early to break open a bottle?' Davidson asked.

'It's never too early for that,' Haynes replied.

Davidson went to the drinks cabinet.

'A nice white from the Western Cape,' he said.

Chapter 2

'Listen, Haynes,' he said. 'Do I understand you rightly? Do you mean that you would be willing to do something dangerous?'

'Yes.'

'And illegal?'

'Yes.'

'Yes, yes!' Haynes said, beating the palm of one hand with his clenched fist. 'Give me a chance of something big, Malcolm. Remember what I told you. Twelve months.......'

'You misunderstand,' Davidson said slowly. 'What I'm going to suggest to you may seem difficult enough, and, under the circumstances, unpleasant, but there is no actual risk - at least,' he corrected himself, 'there shouldn't be.'

Haynes laughed scornfully. 'For God's sake, spit it out, man. If the thing is big enough, I'm not afraid. If it's dishonest, say so.'

Davidson was silent for several moments. It was a chance, this, - just a chance. He looked out of the window, and he seemed to see all the splendid details of his rise to power. And he remembered that in business, houses are often built on clay. In that moment he knew what it would be like to lose everything he'd worked for. There were enemies at his gate. He must fight to the end, make use of any means that came to his hand. It was a chance this, only a chance, but he would take it!

'Listen, Haynes,' he said, 'I'm going to take you at your word. That you mean exactly what you say.'

'God knows I do!' Haynes muttered.

'Very well, then,' Davidson said, 'I want you to understand this. The company of which I'm managing director owns, as you may have heard, some of the most productive mines in the world. We're not Oppenheimer, but we're breathing down their necks.'

'I worked for De Beers in Zambia for a time,' Haynes said.

'Our chief possession,' Davidson continued, 'is the Letlakana Mine, which was once, as you may know, my property. Did you know anything of the history of the Letlakana Mine, Haynes?'

Haynes nodded. 'It was a deserted claim which you and some others were interested in. Dick Tacon was one of them. Austin put you on to it.'

Davidson nodded. 'It was a deserted claim. Four of us took possession, but the other three never knew what I knew. I bought up their shares one by one. The mine grew and prospered. What it has become, you know. I sold it to this corporation. I wished to have no outside interests, and the price paid me was.......well, we're talking big bucks.'

'And?'

'Three weeks ago, where you are sitting now, Haynes, I had another visitor. Richard Austin.'

'That swine!' Haynes said.

'He produced documents, and tried to convince me that he was the real owner of the Letlakana Mine, that it had never been deserted, and that our taking possession of it was nothing more nor less than illegal.'

Haynes was plainly amazed. 'But it was Austin,' he exclaimed, 'who put you on to it in the first place. Wasn't it?'

Davidson nodded. 'That,' he said, 'may have been part of his scheme. He hadn't the money or the patience to work it himself, and it may have occurred to him that if he could get someone else to do all the work, believing that they had acquired the mine, it might be worth his claiming afterwards. I've talked to lawyers. Spent a small fortune talking to South Africa. The conclusion....if Austin prosecutes his claim - and he means business - and goes to law, there is just a reasonable chance he might win.'

'A reasonable chance,' Haynes repeated.

'It isn't only that, though,' continued Davidson. 'There are other things to be taken into consideration. We don't want a lawsuit. Several of our smaller mines are doing rather badly just now, and we have been spending an immense amount of money on developments. Any suspicion as to the validity of our title to the Letlakana Mine would be absolutely disastrous. Our shares would plummet, just at the time when we are least prepared for it.'

'Where do I come in?' Haynes said quietly.

'Austin,' Davidson said, 'is staying at the Universal Hotel, where I imagine that he spends most of his time poolside, drinking beer. Now I can't parley with the fellow, Haynes. That's the trouble. If I were to show the least sign of weakness, the game would be up. My only chance was bluff. I laughed in his face and turned him out of the office. But bluff doesn't alter facts.'

'Austin has a damned good claim,' Haynes thought, but said nothing.

'You and he are old acquaintances. I know very well that you never hit it off together, although I never knew the cause of your quarrel.'

Davidson waited for a confidence but Haynes wasn't going to be drawn.

There's nothing to stop me going to see him,' Haynes said.

'Exactly! Find out whether this is a put-up thing or whether he actually believes.....'

Haynes nodded. 'Anything else?' he said in a low voice.

'There is no reason,' Davidson continued, 'why you should not, if he gets confidential, open up negotiations on your own account.'

'He has some documents, I suppose?' Haynes said.

'His claim to our mine,' Davidson said, 'is contained in a single document, which he told me never left his person. You're a man of the world, Haynes. You know how to argue, to handle facts, to make a bargain. The return of that document to me would be worth fifty thousand bucks.'

'Fifty grand,' Haynes muttered.

'Yes, fifty big ones,' Davidson said.

'Fifty thousand bucks!' Haynes said. 'It would be enough - more than enough.'

'For a single document.'

Then Haynes's face betrayed a cunning look.

'It sounds too good to be true,' Haynes said.

It's lekker,' Davidson replied. 'But if you fail, and find yourself in trouble, I know nothing of you. Haven't seen you in years. You never came to this office. I'll not raise a finger to help you.'

'Fair enough,' Haynes said.

'I must insist......you deal with Austin simply as an old comrade.'

'A speculative financier,' Haynes said.

He smiled. He had in his life been many things but not that.

'Running expenses? I'll need to look presentable.'

'Five grand up front,' Davidson said.

Now Haynes grimaced. 'Cheque. Paper trail. Not a good thing.'

'Cash,' Davidson said. 'No invoices, no receipts.'

'Sounds good. Cash does it for me.'

'Then you're in?'

'Austin played a dirty trick on me once. I've never forgiven him for that.'

'No mention of my name, mind,' Davidson repeated emphatically.

The two men shook hands. The deal was done.

Chapter 3

A few hours later, Malcolm Davidson sat with the father of the young woman to whom he had become engaged. His hostess, Lady Linton, and her daughter, Catherine, had only just left them. It had been a dinner en famille.

'Draw up your chair, Malcolm, and try some of this port,' Sir Andrew Linton said.

'Thank you,' replied Davidson. 'I'll finish my champagne, if I may.'

'Just as you like,' his host said. 'Never mix, eh? Perhaps you're right. There's nothing like being absolutely fit, and you fellows in the city have to keep fit.'

Davidson nodded his agreement.

Sir Andrew Linton lit a cigar.

'There was time a fellow asked the father for a girl's hand. But those days have gone.'

Still, Malcolm Davidson kept quiet.

'You won't be surprised I've had you checked out.'

'I'd do the same,' Davidson said.

He smiled. His manner was natural enough, but only he knew how difficult he found it to continue this sort of conversation with his prospective father-in-law.

'I gather your companies are doing rather well.'

Time was, Davidson would have lapped this up but now he strove not to show his apprehension.

Now, the rock upon which it had all been built seemed to have become shifting sand. Dick Austin had changed everything. The document he had boasted of was worthless, of course, but mud, once thrown, sticks.

'Of course, I'm glad enough for Catherine to marry a rich man,' Sir Andrew Linton continued bluntly. 'I warn you,' he said laughing, 'she'll be high maintenance.'

'I'm a little run down, I admit,' Davidson said. 'I'm going to take a holiday in a few weeks.'

'Good for you. Catherine coming with you?'

I invited her, but she's up to the eyebrows with her own work.'

'We have a place in Scotland, if you want to get away from it all.'

'Kind of you, Andrew. Very kind But I need sunshine. And there's a bit of business to conclude in Johannesburg.'

'Well, South Africa's got plenty of that. Sunshine. As well as thieving and violence.'

There was a soft tap on the door. Catherine's head appeared round it.

'Come on, you two.'

'On our way,' Andrew Linton said.

Catherine entered the room

'Daddy talks too much,' she said.

Davidson and Catherine contrived to be alone together in another part of the house

'I have barely an hour, Malcolm,' she said. 'It was absurd of you to be sitting there talking to Daddy all the time. Come and say nice things to me.'

He held her at arm's length, looking at her. She was tall, slim, and graceful. There was about her a sort of groomed perfection, belied by a measure of coldness in her eyes and manner.

Davidson stooped to kiss her.

'You look lovely, darling. I want to get you into bed.'

There isn't time,' Catherine said.

'There's always time for a quickie,' Davidson said.

'Quickie? What sort of language is that? You have a quite vulgar steak, you know. It upsets me.'

'It's meant to excite you, darling,' Davidson said.

And who was she to talk about vulgar streaks in that way? He had had her father checked, knew exactly where he had come from, and how he had made his money. The knighthood was not for anything charitable, nor for some special accomplishment. It was a reward for donations to the Conservative Party.

He ran his fingers across Catherine's breasts.

'You won't expect too much of me in this way, Malcolm, will you?' she said. 'I'm busy most days.'

'No more than five times in every twenty-four hours,' he replied.

'Oh, God, what am I getting myself into?'

'You won't find me exacting,' he said, with a reassuring nod, as he unzipped her dress down the back.

He needed a woman to help him release the tensions and pressures of business, and a presentable hostess. Well, Catherine fitted the bill in both ways.

Later, talking to Sir Andrew Linton again, Davidson was shown the newspaper.

'Chap found dead in his hotel. Sounds like the beginning of a joke, doesn't it?

'Nobody we know, I guess,' Davidson said.

'Supposed to have had a lot of money in his pocket. Found dead in his room at about seven o'clock last night.'

A sudden shiver ran down Davidson's spine.

'Does it name the hotel?' Davidson said.

Sir Andrew Linton glanced at the paper which he still held in his hand. 'The Universal,' he said, 'that huge new place, you know, top end of Piccadilly.'

'Was the murderer caught?' Davidson said.

'Arrested just as he was leaving the hotel,' Sir Andrew Linton said, 'Here's the paper, if you have a taste for horrors.'

Davidson did his best to display no reaction to what he read.

'Nothing wrong, I hope, Malcolm?' Linton said. 'You didn't know the fellow, by any chance, did you?'

Davidson shook his head. He spoke very quietly and very distinctly. Except that he was unusually pale, his manner showed no signs of emotion. And yet, all the time he felt that he was being stifled! In his ears was the deep singing voice of tragedy!

'No!' he said. 'I never heard of him in my life.'

'Stay and have a smoke with me,' Sir Andrew Linton suggested. 'I'm going round to the club in about an hour's time, and then I'm going to pick these people up at a ball somewhere.'

'You're very kind,' Davidson said. 'To tell you the truth, I have just remembered a very important letter which I ought to have written.'

He arranged to see Catherine next day, gave her a perfunctory peck on the cheek, and without further ado, drove off.

Chapter 5

A stream of people came out from the dark forbidding-looking building into the street. The tragedy was over, and one by one they took their several ways, and were swallowed up in the restless life of the great city. Yet there was not one of them who did not carry in his face some trace of those hours of gloomy excitement, some reminiscent shadow of the tragedy which had spread itself out into passionate life before their eyes. The most callous was conscious of a few minutes' unusual gravity. Some of the more impressionable carried with them the memory of that hot, crowded room, the air of tense excitement, the slowly spoken, solemn words, throughout that day and many days to come.

'And may the Lord have mercy upon your soul!'

There was one man who issued from the building and made his way into the street, who seemed altogether dazed. His lips were drawn tightly together, his eyes were set in an unseeing stare. It was not until he had walked fifty yards or so that he seemed even to realize where he was. Then he came to a sudden standstill, and retraced his steps. Standing outside the building which he had just quitted was a small electric taxi, in front of which he stopped. He glanced at his watch. It was a few minutes past one o'clock. All around was the great stream of city men and clerks, hurrying to their mid-day meal. Once more, as he stood with the handle in his hand, he looked back down the dark passage, guarded by a single policeman, through which he had come a moment or two before. The scene in the little courthouse spread itself out with almost hideous precision before his reluctant eyes. Davidson knew tragedy when he witnessed it. He saw a man stand up and listen to the words pronounced which were to deprive him of freedom.

Davidson turned to his chauffeur. 'The Ritz!' he said, and stepped inside.

The taxi glided away, swung in and out of the traffic, and ran smoothly along the Embankment. Davidson let down both the windows, took off his hat and placed it on the seat opposite him. Then he drew a small fine handkerchief from his pocket, and wiped his forehead.

'Good God!' he muttered to himself. 'Twelve men, and not one of them could see the truth. Twelve men, all fools!'

'Stop at the Ritz, Richards,' he ordered.

He pulled up in front of the hotel. Davidson went in hurriedly, exchanging abrupt greetings with one or two acquaintances. There he ordered and drank quickly a large brandy-and-soda. When he retraced his steps, he felt more composed.

'To Wilton's,' he ordered. 'Hurry, please.'

In the foyer of the restaurant, Lady Catherine came slowly forward to meet him. She was beautifully dressed, and she wore her clothes with the air of one who has been accustomed to silk and laces from the days of her cradle. She had been a beauty for so long that no one questioned her looks. It seemed even incredible that she was twenty-nine years old. One realized that she was of the order of women who refuse to grow old, - women without nerves, unruffled by emotions, women who come smiling through the years. To Davidson she had never seemed more desirable than when she greeted him with a slight uplifting of her eyebrows, and turned to present him to another man and woman who were standing by.

'Mr. Davidson is going to make the usual excuses, I know,' she said. 'Let's anticipate him, and say nothing about our wait. We won't even ask whether it was a directors' meeting, or a message from the governor of the Bank of England. Malcolm, this is my cousin, Mary Pyne, and her husband, Major Pyne.'

The man shook hands.

The others are somewhere about,' Catherine said. 'What a tiresome person Julia is! She has drifted away over there with a lot of people whom I don't know. That is the worst of taking Julia anywhere. Do find her, Malcolm. No, don't bother! Here she comes.'

A tall, dark woman detached herself from a neighbouring crowd, and came up to Davidson with outstretched hands. 'My dear Malcolm!' she said 'How dare you look so cool and nonchalant! Do you realize that we are all starving? We have been waiting here for you for more than half an hour.'

'I'm sorry,' Davidson said. 'You see, you people here have taken to having lunch so early nowadays. You make it hard for a man to get through any work at all in the city.'

'Early lunches have come in with the simpler life,' Julia Cooper said. 'One has so many more hours to look forward to dinner, and so much more appetite when it comes. I suppose we must forgive you,' she went on. 'At any rate, you are better than my husband, who won't come out to lunch at all. He says that all restaurant food is poisonous, and I can't drag him away from the club. Why a man should put his digestion before our society, I can't imagine. I hope you will never be so ungallant, Malcolm. Shall we go in, Catherine?'

'If you will excuse me for one moment,' Davidson said, passing on ahead, 'I'll just see that the table is ready. Even a maître forgets sometimes.'

He looked into the room, and nodded to the presiding genius who came hurrying up. The table was there, duly reserved, and covered with the dark red roses which he had ordered. He turned to Mrs. Pyne and the others who were following her.

'I think we can go in,' he said.

Lady Catherine looked at him a little curiously as she took the seat at his left, hers by unspoken consent as his fiancée. 'My dear Malcolm,' she whispered, 'have you had a very trying morning?'

He hesitated. 'Well,' he said, 'I had rather a bad hour or so. Things don't go always our way, you know.'

'You're foolish to worry,' she said calmly. 'Half the people in the world spoil their lives by giving way to that sort of thing. I'd have thought that your temperament would have saved you from that.'

Davidson smiled. 'Remember,' he said, 'that I have been in other places when I might have been with you, and excuse me.'

'You are much too gallant,' she said, with a little laugh, 'to argue with seriously.'

'By the bye,' Major Pyne said, 'I wonder if the Haynes case is finished.'

Davidson spoke. 'The verdict was given just as I left the city,' he said. 'Haynes was found guilty!'

Chapter 6

There was a little murmur of interest. On the whole, although the result of the trial had seemed fairly certain, everyone was surprised.

'Murder or manslaughter?' Major Pyne said.

'Of murder,' Davidson said.

Lady Catherine looked reproachfully at him. 'My dear Malcolm, you really shouldn't have told us at lunch time. If I hadn't been so very hungry, I'm sure it would have taken my appetite away. He was such a good-looking fellow, and he has been so brave all through the trial.'

'Brave? Or callous, do you think?' Major Pyne said.

'Brave, I think,' Julia Cooper said, leaning forward in her place. 'I went to the trial the first day. He followed every question that was said, and he was always making suggestions to his solicitor. I think when one understands like that, when one's intellect is working all the time, that you cannot call it callousness.'

'I agree with you,' Lady Catherine said. 'I was there myself, and except that he looked so ill, he seemed quite indifferent, and absolutely free from nervousness. Yet I'm quite sure that he realized his position. My dear Malcolm, how thoughtful of you to remember. I adore hot lobster, don't you, Julia?'

'Delicious!' Julia said.

'I wonder,' Major Pyne said reflectively, 'what must be the state of mind of a man who has gone through a trial lasting four or five days, and suddenly realizes that it is over and finished, and that he has lost. This poor fellow, for instance. When he woke up this morning, he perhaps hoped to be free to-night, - things went altogether his way yesterday. And instead of being free, he has been taken back to his cell, and knows - even at this minute he is realizing - that he will never leave it again until he leaves it to die. Personally,' he continued, 'I think that the period of time between the pronouncement of a sentence and its execution ought to be swept away. I cannot imagine anything more horrible, especially to a man who has to spend the long nights alone with that one thought racking his brain!'

Lady Catherine laid down her fork. 'My dear Harry,' she said, 'do be a little more considerate. How are we to enjoy our luncheon if we think of that poor man?'

Major Pyne bowed across the table. 'I forgot,' he said. 'Let us enjoy our luncheon, by all means. At the same time, I'm going to drink my first glass of wine to a reprieve. We won't discuss the question of whether he deserves it or not. We will talk instead, if you like, of gowns, and the chances for the Derby. But - I drink my toast.'

'You are very quiet, Malcolm,' Catherine said.

Davidson smiled at her. 'I'm afraid that sometimes when I come away from a maze of figures, my brain, or at any rate my tongue, is not as nimble as it should be. I'll keep pace with you all presently.'

A frock-coated, maître d'hôtel came smiling up and addressed him confidentially. 'Mr. Davidson,' he said, 'you are wanted on the phone.

'Are you sure?' Davidson said, a little doubtfully.

'Quite sure, sir,' the man replied. 'The inquiry was for Mr. Malcolm Davidson.'

Davidson rose to his feet. 'You will excuse me?' he said, turning to his guests.

As he left the room and crossed the hall Davidson was conscious of feeling more than a little puzzled. He was quite certain that he had not told a soul at the office of the Incorporated Mines Association, over which he presided, that he was lunching at the Carlton. He was equally certain that he had not told anyone else. He took up the receiver with some curiosity.

'Who is it?' he said.

'Who are you?' was the reply.

'I'm Malcolm Davidson,' Davidson said. 'Who are you, and what do you want with me? Is it the office?'

'No!' was the reply, in a voice wholly unfamiliar to him. 'It is not the office, Mr. Davidson. It is someone with news for you.'

'News?' Davidson repeated. 'I'd like to know who you are first, and to hear your news afterwards.'

'Who I'm is of no consequence,' was the reply. 'My news is that Brian Haynes has been found guilty, and has been sentenced to twenty years. The verdict has just been pronounced.'

The receiver nearly fell from Davidson's fingers. He restrained himself, however, with an effort. 'Well,' he said, 'what is that to you or to me?'

'That is a matter which we will not discuss over the phone,' was the calm reply. 'I rang you up to tell you this because I thought it was well that you should know quickly. I ask you now what you are going to do.'

Davidson's was the face of a strong man - a man who scarcely knew the meaning of the word 'nerves.' Yet he felt himself struggling with a sudden sense of being stifled. Something seemed to be hammering at his brain. His breath was coming in little sobs. He said this mysterious voice almost incoherently.

'What do you mean? How can it concern me? Tell me who you are at once,' he said.

'It does not matter who I am,' was the reply. 'You have no time to think about that. What you want to realize is that Brian Haynes has been found guilty, and that he'll die in prison very soon unless -'

'Unless what?' Davidson gasped.

'Unless someone intervenes,' was the quiet answer.

'Who could intervene?' he said hoarsely. 'How can anyone intervene?'

'You know,' was the quiet answer.

Davidson staggered out of the phone box with those last words ringing in his ears. He felt dazed, scarcely master of himself. The healthy colour seemed to have been drawn from his cheeks, as he turned mechanically back toward the restaurant. Half-way there, however, he paused. For the moment, he felt it impossible to face his guests. He turned into the little smoking-room and sat down. The place was empty. Even the little bar was deserted. He sat in one of the green leather chairs, his hands clutching the cushioned arms, his eyes fixed steadily upon the wall. Slowly it seemed to fall away - to crumble into nothingness - before his rigid gaze. Again he saw the sombre-looking courthouse, the judge upon the bench, his sphinx-like face set in an attitude of cold attention. He saw the barristers, with their wigs and gowns, the few distinguished strangers upon the bench, the crowd of sightseers behind the barriers. And in the centre of it all - Brian Haynes, his pale face and drawn features standing out vividly against the gloomy background. It was no ordinary trial, this. The subtle, dramatic excitement, which only a question of life or death seems to generate, was throbbing through the dreary court. It was only, comparatively speaking, a few days ago that the man who stood there now waiting to hear his doom had found his way down into the city, and sat in his office, and made his passionate appeal. Davidson's hands gripped the sides of the chair, and his lips moved. He told himself, as he had told himself a hundred times before, that this act was none of his doing, that not a single word of his had suggested or approved of it. He had spoken of arguments, of influence. Was it any responsibility of his that the man who had listened had gone further - had chosen to gamble instead with life and death? Davidson went back through that conversation, word by word. No, he was guiltless! He had not suggested violence! He even told himself that he would not have approved of it. And yet the weight upon his heart was not lightened. The little picture was still there, reproduced with almost photographic exactness. Was it his fancy, or had the trembling man's eyes really turned towards him - had his white lips really framed that passionate, unspoken appeal which seemed to ring in his ears?

Davidson rose to his feet with a little stifled cry. He seemed to understand now how men who were left alone with their thoughts might find madness.

Chapter 7

Davidson found his little party drinking their coffee in the palm lounge. Lady Catherine greeted him with raised eyebrows.

'My dear Malcolm!' she said 'Have you been phoning to the other end of the world?'

'I'm so sorry,' he said, taking the vacant chair by her side. 'I came away from the office feeling that I had forgotten something, and it took me quite a long time to straighten things out. Tell me, what are you all going to do this afternoon?'

'We are going down to the country,' Catherine said. 'There is some tennis, and Dicky's playing polo in the regimental finals. Don't you think that you could take an hour or so off, and come down with us? You really look as though you need some fresh air.'

Davidson shook his head. 'Impossible. I have an appointment in the city at half-past three, and another at four. After that I have at least a hundred letters to dictate.'

'I'm beginning to discover,' Catherine said, with an air of resignation, 'that there are disadvantages in being engaged to a city man.'

Davidson smiled. 'Let us hope,' said he, 'that after you are married you will still regard the situation in the same light. Your friend Julia, for instance, declares that she would never have married anyone who was not kept away from home at regular intervals.'

Lady Catherine leaned a little towards him. After all, he had been very nice. The Pynes had found him delightful, and there was no man in the lounge half so good-looking. She decided to say something charming.

'Julia,' she whispered, 'was never in love with her husband, even before she married him.'

'And you?' Davidson said.

She laughed at him and looked away, but he was suddenly insistent, taking her hand, and forcing her to turn again towards him.

'Tell me,' he said quietly, 'do you really care for me, Catherine? Oh! I know you care enough to justify marrying me, but I mean something different. I mean do you really care in the great fashion, you know, like the people one reads of?'

She looked at him as though he were speaking some foreign language. The earnestness in his face was unmistakable. 'Ah, I wonder!' she said. 'What a very strange question to ask me, Malcolm, just now! Frankly, I don't know. I can only tell you that there is no other man. You are quite alone.'

The others were all discussing some subject of kindred interest. Davidson felt curiously prompted to continue his questioning. His engagement had been such a very matter-of-fact affair. To a certain extent it was understood that he was marrying for position, and she for wealth. And yet in all their conversations they had discreetly concealed the fact. They had told each other that they cared, if not with passion, at least in the most approved manner. There had been no suggestion in their many tête-à-têtes that they were about to embark upon a marriage de convenience.

'Tell me,' Davidson persisted, 'if things should go wrong with me, or if you had met me simply as a struggler, with my feet upon the early rungs of the ladder, - tell me, could you have cared then, do you think?'

She looked at him curiously. There was something in his face which compelled the truth. 'I do not know,' she said. 'Let me think.'

'Think, by all means,' he continued. 'Remember that I was introduced to you, even, as one of the youngest millionaires. Forgive me if I seem egotistical, but I have a fancy to put things plainly. There is a glamour about wealth. I came to you with that glamour about my name. I'm rich, of course, and wealth means power. How much of your affection, Catherine, came out to the man, and how much to the millionaire?'

'You want me to give you a perfectly honest answer?' she said.

'Absolutely,' he assured her. 'Don't be afraid of hurting my vanity. I want nothing but the truth.'

'At first, then,' she told him, 'nothing to the man, and everything to the millionaire. This afternoon,' she continued, 'I rather fancy that the man has the larger share. You are quite a fascinating person, Malcolm, when you choose to make yourself agreeable.'

'You can't accuse me,' he said, 'of making any special efforts in that direction today.'

'No!' she said. 'You were rather quiet, but still you were yourself. Personally, I'm beginning to find something very attractive about a silent man. You speak quite often enough, and what you say is to the point. It seems always to be the pronouncement of the man who knows. You have what Julia calls an air of reserved strength about you, which I fancy that my sex finds a little attractive. Tell me, why all this questioning?'

Davidson looked away - through the cluster of palms into the little smoking-room from which he had issued a few minutes before.

'Even the houses,' he said, 'which according to the injunctions of Scripture are built upon a rock, are liable to destruction by earthquakes. So, even, the strongest of us in the city have always the hundredth chance working in the world against us. The most amazing collapses have taken place. I was really wondering what would happen - how greatly it would affect you - if my riches were to vanish into thin air.'

'What an unpractical person you are this afternoon!' she said, looking at him curiously. 'Supposing I were to sit here and worry about the fit of the dress which Madame Catherine is sending me home this afternoon for the ball to-night. I could make myself miserable in five minutes without the shadow of a reason.'

'Madame Catherine,' he said, 'would deserve bankruptcy if she failed to fit a figure like yours.'

Lady Catherine laughed. 'Really,' she said, 'you are becoming quite a courtier.'

'Dear people,' Julia Cooper said, leaning over, 'if we may bring you back to the mundane world, everybody else is dying to start.'

Lady Catherine made a little grimace, and rose to her feet at once. 'Malcolm and I have only been boring one another because you all seemed so occupied,' she said. 'By all means. It's time we made a move.'

They made their way toward the entrance of the restaurant. Catherine fell back once more with Davidson.

'It's such a nuisance about this wretched dinner to-night,' she said. 'I think it was very bad taste indeed of the Duchess to ask us without you. You won't forget to come in and see me for half-an-hour before we go on to the ball?

'I'll be with you.'

'Where are you dining?' she said.

'At the club, most likely. I never dine out on Wednesdays, if I can help it. We are always so busy. I'll have a quiet, comfortable evening.'

'Au revoir, then!' she said, stepping into one of the two vehicles which were waiting.

Davidson made his farewells to the rest of the party and watched them drive off. Then he called a hansom.

'Messrs. Shackleton and Associates, Bedford Row,' he told the man. 'And I'm in a hurry.'

Chapter 8

John Shackleton, although he was a solicitor in a very busy practice, did not keep his friend waiting. 'Come in, Malcolm, old chap,' he said. 'Is this business or friendship?'

'Mostly business,' Davidson said.

Shackleton glanced at the clock. 'Twelve minutes, precisely,' he said. 'Fire away, there's a good fellow. You're not going to give me the affairs of the Incorporated Mines Association to look after, I suppose?'

'Not I,' Davidson said. 'They need a more subtle brain than yours, I'm afraid. I have come to see you about the other affair.'

The lawyer nodded. 'You heard the result?' he said. 'We did what we could.'

'Perhaps,' Davidson said. 'The only thing is that you did not do enough. I'm perfectly convinced, John, that that man did not go there with the intention of murdering Austin.'

'The evidence,' Shackleton said, 'was exceedingly awkward.'

'Do you think,' Davidson said, 'that there is any chance of an appeal?'

'As things stand at present,' said Shackleton,' 'quite difficult.

Davidson for the first time sat down. With frowning face, he seemed to be engaged in a deliberate study of the pattern of the carpet. 'Shackleton,' he said finally, 'I want to ask you a question in criminal law.'

The lawyer laughed dryly. 'Not on your own account, I hope?'

'You can call it curiosity, or whatever you like,' Davidson said. 'The only point is that I want you to answer me a question, and forget that I have ever said it you. Your lawyer is like your confessor, isn't he - your lawyer and your doctor?'

'He should be,' Shackleton said gravely.

'Then here goes,' Davidson said. 'I put a case to you. I mention no names. You can imagine, if you like, that I'm writing a novel. A man is tried for murder, and he is sentenced to be hanged. All the time there has been watching this case, listening to every word of the evidence, a person who knows quite as much of it as the prisoner himself, - someone who, if it had been possible, could have gone into the witness box and could very likely have induced the jury to have reduced the charge from murder to manslaughter. Never mind the reasons which made that man hold his tongue. Consider only the fact that he did hold his peace, believing in his heart that it was not possible, on the evidence which was submitted, for the man to be sentenced. As it happened, the case for the prosecution was worked up with almost diabolical cleverness, and the prisoner was found guilty - guilty of murder. He was sentenced to be hanged. What can this person do to save his life? The trial is closed. It is too late for him to offer himself as a witness.'

Shackleton nodded. 'I understand,' he said. 'The procedure is very simple. He should go to the solicitors for the defence, and they will communicate with the Home Secretary.'

'The case cannot be reopened?' Davidson said.

'No!' said Shackleton, with a shake of the head. 'Our criminal law has many anomalies. The only thing that could happen in the prisoner's favour would be that if this favourable evidence were convincing enough, the prisoner might be granted a free pardon, and the facts made known through the Press. Anything more I can tell you?'

'Nothing,' Davidson said, rising. 'Many thanks, old fellow. You have told me just what I want to know.'

'The only real chance of a review of sentence,' Shackleton continued, 'is on account of the fellow's health. I believe he is really very much worse than he appears, and I fancy that if we had a medical examination it would give us at least a chance. The trouble is that he really seems quite indifferent. Are you thinking of trying to see him?'

Davidson shook his head. 'No!' he said. 'I'm afraid I must not do that. There are reasons why I dare not let my name be associated in any way with this affair. They may come out later on, but just at present I would rather not tell even you what they are. By the bye, has anyone representing the dead man turned up at all - I mean has anyone claimed his effects?'

'No one,' the lawyer said. 'From what I can learn they are very insignificant.'

Davidson nodded. 'Can I rely upon you,' he said, 'to let me know at once if anyone should come forward to claim them?'

'By all means,' Shackleton said.

Davidson went out into the street, and stood there for a few moments a little aimlessly. Then he called a cab and was driven to his offices, a great block of buildings like a bank, situated in a small court off Throgmorton Street. He passed through the outer offices slowly, asking several questions, and shaking hands with one or two acquaintances. When at last he reached the inner room, his own sanctum, he turned out his secretary ruthlessly, and locked the door. He sat in his leather chair in front of the open table, covered with letters and books of reference. It was before this table that he had built up the fortunes of the great corporation at whose head he was. He sat there now, erect in his chair, with his hands stretched out on the table before him, and his eyes looking through the frosted panes of glass opposite. Was there any compromise, he said himself, - any possible compromise? Again he was looking into the gloomy court. Again he saw the white face of the man who so short a time ago had sat in this very room, only a few feet away, and had begged so hard for his chance! The whole scene came flashing back to Davidson as he sat there. How much of blame, after all, was his? He had not suggested violence. He refused even to admit that it had entered into his head. Yet he had known what manner of men these two were! He had known, and their meeting had been all his making! Never in this world would he be able to escape from the responsibility of it, -

never in this world would he be able to hear those awful words without a sense of real and personal guilt, - 'And may the Lord have mercy upon your soul!'

Chapter 9

The clerk who brought in the little slip of paper was both timid and apologetic. He felt himself between two fires. The young lady outside had been a little more than insistent. The man into whose presence he had come was one who never forgave a mistake.

'You will pardon me, sir,' he said. 'I hope that I have not done wrong. The young lady outside positively declined to go away until she had seen you. I thought that I had better at least bring you in her name. I remembered that a few weeks ago you saw a gentleman of the same name, although it was one of your busiest mornings.'

Davidson held out his hand, frowning. 'A young lady,' he said shortly. 'Well?'

He took the little slip of paper into his hands, and read - Eileen Haynes. He looked up into the clerk's impassive face, and back again at the slip of paper. 'The young lady is waiting outside?' he said.

'She is outside, sir,' the clerk said. 'I explained to her that you were not in the habit of seeing any callers except by appointment, and I begged her to write and fix a time, if she really had business with you. She said, however, that the matter was an urgent one. Mr. Sawyer and I both heard what she had to say, sir, and we thought it best that I'd bring you in her name.'

Davidson nodded slowly. 'I dare say you were right, ,' he said. 'Since the young lady is so persistent, you had better show her in. See that I'm not disturbed again this afternoon, however. I have a good deal to do.'

The clerk departed with a great weight off his mind. It was obvious that he had done the right thing. He left the door ajar, and Davidson sat with his hands clenching the sides of his luxuriously padded writing chair. Eileen Haynes! It was a relative, then, - most likely the sister of whom he had spoken. What was he to say or do? How much was he to admit? Perhaps she had brought him a message. Perhaps she could tell him the one thing which he was on fire to know. Eileen Haynes! Half unconsciously he uttered the name aloud. What sort of a woman would she be, or girl, or child? He had no knowledge of Haynes save as a fellow adventurer, a seeker after fortune in a strange land, a brave man, willing always to take his life into his hands if the goal were worthy. Perhaps it might be that she had been with him. Perhaps she was bringing a message.

He heard the murmur of voices outside. The door was pushed open. The clerk stood on one side.

'This is the young lady, sir,' he announced, - 'Miss Eileen Haynes.'

Davidson rose for a moment to his feet. The clerk, with a little deferential movement, closed the door and departed. They were alone in the room together. Davidson, whose self-control was one of the personal characteristics which had counted for something in his rapid access to prosperity, felt a nerveless exclamation break from his lips. The girl who came so slowly into the room seemed so perfectly to represent what Haynes himself might have become. She was an idealized likeness of the man by whose side he had fought and suffered and rejoiced, the man who only a few weeks ago had stood in her place and made his desperate appeal, - an idealized likeness, perhaps, in more ways than one. She was younger, and the stress of life had only lately set its mark upon her. She was fair, as he was fair, with blue eyes, brown hair, and quivering lips, a figure slim and yet pliant, a manner, even in silence, appealing, - enticing. Davidson felt himself curiously moved at the sight of her. Then he remembered suddenly how great was his need of self-control. She was the sister of this man who lay under sentence of life imprisonment. Perhaps she had come to plead for his help. He must be careful. All the time he must be careful!

'You wish to see me?' he said, a little brusquely. 'I'm Malcolm Davidson. Will you take a chair, and tell me in as few words as you can what you want?'

She ignored his gesture of invitation. She came on until she had reached the table before which he was seated. Then she leaned across, and the light of her eyes, the very insistence of her presence, seemed like things from which no escape was possible.

'Mr. Davidson,' she said, 'I'm Brian Haynes's sister. I have come from the Old Bailey prison. I have come,' she added, with faltering voice, and a sudden new terror in her face, 'from the condemned cell.'

Davidson had a reserve stock of courage to draw upon, and he drew upon it freely. He looked at her with upraised eyebrows. 'You have come to me,' he repeated. 'Why?'

'First of all, then,' she said, 'I will tell you why.'

'I think,' he interrupted, 'that you had better take a seat.'

She seemed, indeed, in need of some support. She sank into the chair which he had indicated. It was close to his side, and yet placed so that the light which fell upon her face left him in the shadow.

'You have come from your brother,' he said. 'Do I understand that he sent you - that he knew you were coming to me?'

'Yes!' she said. 'He told me to be very careful, to be sure that no one else knew, and never to mention your name, but I have come at his bidding.'

'Very well,' Davidson said, 'I'll be glad to hear your message.'

'He gave me no explanation,' she said. 'He allowed me to ask for none. He told me to come to you and say this. There is no one,' she said, in a lower tone, looking nervously around, 'who could possibly overhear us?'

'Not a soul.'

'He told me to say,' she continued, leaning forward, and with her eyes suddenly a little distended, 'that he had no difficulty in finding the man of whom you two had spoken - the man whom you used to call Bully Austin . He spent the evening with him, drank with him, went back to his hotel by invitation. Then he tried very carefully to open up negotiations. Austin became at once suspicious. He was very violent, and declined to discuss the matter at all. He swore all the time that he had been robbed, and that he was going to have his revenge. My brother tried to reason with him, and in the end they quarrelled. It was Austin who struck Brian. My brother only said the blow. And then he told me to say that before he could search him, before he could search the room, he found that the man was dead.'

'Anything else?' Davidson said.

'He told me to say that any papers which the man Austin might have had must be in the room among his effects, which have all been put together, and are still there, locked up, waiting for someone to come and claim them. He told me to say that he had done his best, and that whatever the consequences might be he was ready to face them. If you cared to run risks, the number of the room at the Universal Hotel is 27. It is locked and guarded, but there might be ways. That is what he said.'

Davidson leaned a little forward across the table. 'But of himself?' he said. 'Did he say nothing of himself?'

She shook her head. 'It is wonderful,' she said, 'but he never thinks of himself. He is more composed, more cheerful, than when I bade him good-night at Southampton, the day he left home. He made me promise that I would tell you these things first, before I uttered a word on my own account. I have kept my promise. You understand what I have told you?'

'Perfectly,' Davidson said.

'Then I'm going to speak to you now on my own account,' she said, raising her eyes to his. 'Mr. Davidson, I do not pretend to be a clever person, but one thing is perfectly clear to me. Brian entered into this adventure for your sake. Your name was never mentioned in the trial, and they all seem to have believed that it was to rob Austin, and for nothing else, that Brian went there that night. Mr. Davidson, I don't believe it. His quarrel with Austin, and its awful termination, was an accident. You must come forward and say that he went there to serve you, and not for purposes of robbery. It is for you to save his life. You can do it. He is my only brother.'

Davidson's eyebrows came a little closer together. The girl who looked at him wondered no more at the hopeless way in which her brother had spoken of this man. His face was as though it were carved out of a stone.

'Miss Haynes,' he said, 'if there is anything which I can do for your brother, I will do it, for the sake of the days when we lived together, and when we were so near the very heart of life and death. But I tell you frankly that I see very little chance of successful intervention on my part. It takes a good deal in this country to stay the arm of the law, and your brother has grievously offended against it.'

She struck the table before which he sat, with the palm of her hand. 'If he did,' she cried, 'it was for your sake! I'm sure of it! He went to do your bidding, and you must save him!'

'May I ask,' Davidson said, 'why you are so sure that he went to do my bidding?'

'Yes! Ask, if you will, and I will answer you. I know it because this was the real point of all his message to you. This was what I had to say. This is really why I have come. The document - the document, mind, - he said no more, but he told me to make this very clear to you - the document is in a worn leather case, sewn inside the breast pocket of the coat Austin was wearing when he died.'

Davidson drew a little breath. 'Young lady,' he said, 'it seems to me that you have been unnecessarily prolix. Your brother sent you here to tell me this?'

'Yes!'

'He did not send you here,' Davidson continued, 'to beg for help - to waste my time in purposeless recriminations?'

'No!' she said faintly.

'He knew very well,' Davidson continued, 'that no mortal man can help him. The trial is over and the case is lost. The only thing to work for now is a reprieve.'

'But that isn't what I want,' she interrupted. 'He must be released!'

'That,' Davidson said, 'is impossible. Neither I nor anyone breathing can work miracles.'

She leaned towards him with accusing eyes. 'But it was you,' she said, - 'it was you for whom he undertook this enterprise!'

Davidson shrugged his shoulders. 'My dear young lady,' he said, 'you are mistaken. I cannot explain to you yet the full significance of those various messages which you have brought me from your brother, but believe me, what he did, he did knowing well the risks he undertook, and without any thought or hope of aid from me if he should fail. I will be quite honest with you, if you like. I will tell you the exact truth. Your brother and Austin were once friends. Austin and I were always enemies. There was a little matter of business open

50

between us, and I thought that your brother might very well arrange it. I had no idea of his quarrelling with Austin. I didn't encourage him in any way.'

'You sent him there,' she persisted doggedly.

'I send messengers to every part of the world,' Davidson said, 'but I don't incite them to enter into murderous quarrels with the people whom they go to see. I will do what I can for your brother, but it must be in my own way.'

'You will be able at least to save him from - from -'

Davidson held out his hand. 'Of course,' he said. 'You need not think about that. His health alone would be sufficient to put that out of the question. What I can do for him, I will. I promise you that.'

The girl rose, and held out her hands a 'Remember, I have no one else to go to, no other hope but in you. If I lose Brian, I'll be alone in the world!'

Tears were in her eyes. Every line of her face, every feature, pleaded with him. Davidson led her to the door. His tone was unusually kind.

'I'll do my best,' he said.

Chapter 10

The door had barely closed upon his visitor when Davidson was back once more in the throes of business, answering questions, giving quotations, receiving offers. The line was reconnected, and rang out its impatient summons every few seconds. He signed half-a-dozen drafts, deputed an understudy to receive some of his visitors who were weary of waiting, and dictated several important letters. When once more the pressure had abated, and the phone had ceased to ring, he leaned back in his chair with a little exclamation of relief. The visit of Haynes's sister, and her passionate appeal, had unnerved him for a moment. He found himself trying to recall her last words, even at the moment when he realized that she was still in the room, sitting at a distant corner.

'Miss Haynes!' he said 'Why, I thought that you had left!'

'I went as far as the outer office,' she said apologetically, 'and then I slipped back again. You were so busy that I did not like to interrupt.'

Davidson rose to his feet, - he was a little cramped from long sitting. He lowered the blind and turned on the electric light, walking around the room, and casually touching the door to see that it was closely shut. Then he came back to his place, and leaned over once more toward the girl. 'Why have you come back?' he said.

'To ask you a question,' she said.

'Well?'

'Brian went on your behalf to see this man, Austin,' she said. 'He had a commission from you, had he not, and he failed?'

'Yes!' Davidson said. 'He failed!'

'It was to make an offer for some document, was it not?' Davidson nodded. 'Yes!' he said. 'It was.'

'You are doing your best for Brian,' she said, her voice trembling a little. 'You paid for his defence, I know. You have promised that you will do all that you can, even now. I thought, perhaps, I might be able to do something in return. Why couldn't I get this paper for you?'

He looked at her steadily for several moments. 'You could,' he said, 'if you had the pluck.'

'Tell me how?' she said.

'You are his sister,' he said. 'Presumably you are interested in his defence. The details of the struggle between those two are, of course, important. It makes all the difference between manslaughter and murder if a weight, for instance, be held in the hand or thrown. You know the lawyers who defended him?'

'Of course,' she said. 'Go on.'

'If they apply to the proper authorities,' he continued, 'they can obtain an order to re-examine the apartments in the Universal Hotel in which the struggle took place. No doubt you also could find your way there. Supposing I tell you the truth. Supposing I admit that your brother did take upon himself a desperate enterprise, and that that enterprise was to recover from this man Austin, by purchase or guile, or any means which suggested themselves to him, the pocket-book of which you have brought me news. Remember I commit myself to nothing. I make no definite statement. I simply tell you that it may have been so.'

'It was,' she said firmly. 'You and I know that. Well?'

'You are his sister,' Davidson said, 'and you have exceptional facilities. If you could gain possession of that pocket-book, you would be doing me a service which I'd find it hard indeed to repay.'

She rose to her feet. 'Very well,' she said, 'it shall be done. I promise you that it shall be done.'

For the first time, when he saw her standing up, and realized how frail a creature she really was, a wave of pity swept away his own predominant sense of self-interest.

'But you're not right for such work as this,' he said. 'Better let things drift. I can take care of myself.'

She shook her head. 'I have made up my mind,' she said. 'I'm going to make my effort, whatever happens.'

'You will remember,' he said, 'that my name must never pass your lips. No, don't look at me like that!' he added quickly. 'Don't think of me as a coward, or an utterly selfish person! I'm here for what I represent. Welfare in this concern or business undertaking - call it what you like - doesn't mean only ruin or wealth for me. There are hundreds of us, hundreds who are dependent upon the reins I hold. It isn't for myself so much that I care. Try and believe that, will you?'

She looked into his eyes. 'I will,' she said. 'I will believe everything, but you must save Brian.'

'Whether you bring me the pocket-book or not,' he said, 'I'll assuredly do all that a man can do for him.'

For the rest of the day, Malcolm Davidson was his normal self. He transacted business with his usual acumen. He received his callers, and went through the ordinary routine of his position, with no indication of any mental disturbance. He had, indeed, little time to spare for thought. At half-past six he was whirled away westward in his electric taxi, changed his clothes, dined hurriedly in his room, and at a quarter to nine was in the stalls of the St. James' Theatre, sitting between Lady Catherine and her mother. The mechanical part of the day's arrangements he had found it easy enough to carry out, but to keep his thoughts engrossed upon his surroundings was a sheer impossibility. He was not even conscious when the curtain went down, until he found Catherine's eyes fixed curiously upon him.

'Malcolm,' she said, 'I don't think I like you when you have been at the office all day. Tell me, what can there be about this money-making so engrossing that you carry it about with you after you have finished your work, like a shadow?'

He was at once duly apologetic. 'My dear,' he said, 'if I was somewhere else for a moment, please forgive me. Consider. It is not my occupation alone which is engrossing. Supposing, for instance, that I were a politician. Don't you think that I'd be better employed in thinking over an impending crisis than in listening to an exceedingly dull play?'

'Perhaps,' she admitted, 'but crises do not occur in political affairs every day. I might even be vain enough to suggest another and a simpler means of escape from your boredom.'

'I'm very justly rebuked,' he admitted, holding her fingers for a moment, 'only you must remember that it is new for me to have so delightful a means of escape ready by my side. Give me a little time to realize my good fortune.'

'So long as it doesn't become a habit,' she said. 'I'm sure I'm not exacting, but I'd hate to feel that you were always so engrossed in your thoughts that you did not even realize whom you were sitting next.'

He touched her fingers once more, and his pressure was gently said. Then, as if conscious that she had been a little more than ordinarily complacent, she withdrew her hand, and leaning over began to talk with her mother about some people whom Davidson knew nothing of. A man from behind touched him on the shoulder. He looked up quickly and recognized Shackleton.

'Come and have a drink,' the lawyer said. 'It is a quarter of an hour's interval, and I'd like to have a word with you.'

Davidson excused himself to his companions, and joined his friend in the foyer. 'Well?' he said tersely.

Shackleton was tall and thin, clean-shaven, with hard, pronounced features and sunken eyes, grey hair parted in the middle, and a single eyeglass suspended around his neck by a narrow black ribbon. He looked exactly what he was - a criminal lawyer.

'I wanted to have a word with you, Davidson,' he said, 'about this Haynes case.'

Davidson nodded. 'Is there anything fresh?' he said.

'Nothing particular,' the lawyer said. 'Come upstairs for a moment.'

They found a corner of the refreshment room where no one else was within hearing. There was nothing in his face to indicate the fierce anxiety which was consuming him.

'With reference to that case,' his companion started, 'the facts were all so simple that there was no need for the prosecution to consider any other motive than the obvious one of attempted robbery. Therefore, no very searching investigation has been made into the dead man's papers. Yesterday afternoon, it occurred to me to look them through once more, in case anything had been overlooked. I came across a clumsy sort of document purporting to be the deeds of a Mine. I'd not have taken any particular notice of it but for the title of the mine.'

'Well?'

'It was the Letlakana Mine,' Shackleton continued. 'These deeds stated that Austin himself was the sole owner.'

'A very extraordinary document,' Davidson said. 'I suppose you couldn't manage things so that I could have a look at it?'

'It would be quite impossible,' the lawyer said. 'Mine was, of course, a privileged inspection, and I'm going beyond my duty in mentioning this affair to you. It certainly did seem very singular.'

'Especially,' Davidson said, with a faint, hard smile, 'since you are in a position to know that I have paid for the defence of the prisoner.'

'It is not my business to connect such facts,' the lawyer said.

'Someone will appear upon the scene sooner or later, of course,' Davidson said, 'and claim this man's effects.'

'Naturally,' Shackleton said, 'although, except for this rather remarkable document, they do not seem to have been very valuable.'

'If you should hear of anyone,' Davidson said, 'I'd be glad if you would let me know without delay.'

'I will do so,' the lawyer promised.

The bell tinkled. The men at the bar finished their drinks and hurried off. Davidson and his companion rose to their feet.

'Shackleton,' Davidson said, 'some of the papers are talking about a reprieve for this man Haynes. Will it come to anything, do you think?'

'I don't know,' the lawyer said cautiously.

They moved along the passage leading down to the stalls. Davidson held his companion back until the little throng of hurrying men had passed by.

'Listen, Shackleton,' he said, 'I speak to you as one speaks to the dead, because you know the secrets of your profession, and because I trust you. Is there any way in which a man of great wealth, who had the command of money say up to fifty thousand pounds, - is there any way in which such a man could help towards obtaining a reprieve?'

Shackleton hesitated for a moment. 'Of course,' he admitted, 'influence is always a useful thing. Those who have the ruling of these matters are sometimes hesitating between two minds. A very straw might turn the balance.'

Davidson nodded his head. He looked for a moment behind. His hand rested upon the curtain which led into the stalls. There was not a soul in sight. The play had restarted.

'Shackleton,' he said, 'I will give fifty thousand pounds, if necessary, to have that man reprieved. The verdict should have been one of manslaughter. I'm convinced of that. I was in court. I heard the sentence. I saw Haynes's face. I watched as the judge read out the sentence.'

Lady Catherine was almost petulant. 'What a time you have been, Malcolm!' she said.

'I met a man outside who kept me gossiping about trifles. Tell me, do you think that we can persuade your mother to come out to supper?'

'We've nowhere else to go,' Lady Catherine said. 'Do see if you can talk her into it. It would be very pleasant.'

'I'll try,' he promised.

Chapter 11

A tabloid paper, apparently in need of a new sensation, suddenly took up the cause of Brian Haynes. An evening paper, conducted under the same auspices, promptly followed suit. This was a case, they both said, of obvious manslaughter. The evidence clearly pointed to a quarrel between the two men. A prominent criminal lawyer allowed his name to be associated with what rapidly grew to be an agitation. Petitions began to appear. The Home Secretary was bombarded with documents. Everywhere people were saying that the man should never have been put on his trial for murder. The jury had been confused by their instructions. It was a case of manslaughter, pure and simple.

Three days after her first visit, Eileen Haynes sat once more in Davidson's office. There were lines underneath her eyes. She seemed to have become thinner and more fragile. Davidson himself, save that he was a trifle paler, was unchanged, - carefully dressed as usual, and with unruffled demeanour. He sat in his accustomed place, and guided the destinies of those great affairs which lay under his control. For the moment he had relaxed. He was doing his best to console the girl who had come to him in a sudden whirl of terror.

'My dear Miss Haynes,' he said, 'I have certain intelligence from my friends. I've gone to great lengths in this matter, and I can assure you that there isn't the slightest doubt about a reprieve being forthcoming.'

She glanced at the calendar. 'But think,' she said, 'already for three days he has been there. Think of what he must be suffering.'

He held out his hand. She was on the verge of hysteria. 'It won't come,' he said firmly. 'I have promised you that.'

'If they are going to reprieve him,' she continued, 'why do they let him suffer these agonies? Why not tell him so at once? I saw him this morning. He says nothing. He is as brave as a man can be, but his eyes are awful, and when he tries to speak his voice dies away. Oh! Mr. Davidson, do something! Oh! do something!'

She laid her hands suddenly upon his shoulders. He took them gently in his.

'My dear Miss Haynes, I'm doing everything that a man can do. Believe me that I'm.....I only wish that your brother had done as he threatened, and walked into the river, before he came to me.'

She went away at last. Davidson lay back in his chair, feeling absolutely unfit for work. Twice he laid his hand upon the phone, and twice he withdrew it. Then he turned to his secretary, who had just entered the room.

'Get Shackleton on the phone,' he directed. 'I want to speak to him.'

There was no delay.

'This is Malcolm Davidson. You remember the subject of our conversation the other night at the theatre? I'm referring now to the matter of documents of which you spoke.'

'I remember,' Shackleton said.

'Who has those documents at the present moment?' Davidson said.

'In whose possession,' Shackleton repeated. 'Do you mean -?'

'I mean have they been sent to Scotland Yard, or are they still in that locked-up room at the Universal Hotel?'

There was a moment's pause. Then Shackleton said. 'To the best of my belief,' he said, 'they are still in the room at the hotel. They may be removed to Scotland Yard at any time, though.'

'No one has yet claimed Austin's effects, then?' Davidson said.

'No one,' was the answer.

Davidson was on the point of ringing off, but Shackleton suddenly put a question to him. 'Will you be in your office for ten minutes, Mr. Davidson?'

'For longer than that,' Davidson said.

'I'm coming around,' the lawyer said. 'I hope you can spare me a moment.'

Davidson set down the phone with a frown. Perhaps his question had been a clumsy one, or was Shackleton already suspicious? He welcomed the lawyer, when he arrived, a little coldly.

'Five minutes, please,' he said. 'I have a large mail to go through, and an early dinner-party to-night.'

The lawyer nodded. 'I don't want to detain you, Davidson,' he said. 'Send your secretary away for a moment, there's a good fellow. What I have to say can be said in half-a-dozen words if we are alone.'

Davidson pointed to the door. 'One moment, if you please, Ellison,' he said. 'Get everything ready for me that you can.'

The two men were now alone. Shackleton, who had not taken a seat, deliberately drew off his glove, and tapped the table with his fingertips.

'Davidson,' he said, 'have you any idea of paying a visit to the Universal Hotel?'

Davidson met him on his own ground, coolly, and with perfect self-possession. 'I haven't made up my mind,' he said. 'It might be worth it.'

'It wouldn't,' the lawyer said. 'There's nothing haphazard about the way these things are conducted. There's a detective watching Number 27, day and night.'

'It occurred to me,' Davidson said, 'that as there is no mystery about this affair, Scotland Yard wouldn't have thought that necessary.'

'It is as I have told you,' said Shackleton. 'At any time after tomorrow, the man's clothing and documents, and everything belonging to him, will be removed, unless they are claimed. Until they are claimed they are watched. It wouldn't do, Davidson, for a man in your position to be seen in this place, especially when one of those papers bears the name of your mine, and Austin has just been murdered by a man for whose defence you have paid.'

'That's plain speaking,' Davidson said.

'It's what I came to say,' Shackleton said. 'Don't do it, Davidson. This is not Africa, you know. Your methods were splendid there. They might spell ruin here. Good-night!'

'The reprieve?' Davidson said.

'A certainty,' Shackleton said, looking back from the door. 'It may be a week before it is issued, but it is a certainty all the same.'

Davidson sat in his chair, looking through the large window out into the court. Of the lawyer's words he took little enough notice. The reprieve would come, of that he was certain, but nevertheless he was beginning to feel the severity of the strain. He was a man who would have been kind-hearted but for the continual pressure of business obligations. He was a great schemer, a man of imagination, and a brilliant financier. There had been little room in his life for the gentler side of his nature to develop. Yet it had been a genuine horror which he had felt, which he had carried about with him since the day he had visited the court and looked into Haynes's white face, and heard those awful words of condemnation amid a silence intense, unnatural, hideous. It was a memory from which he could not easily rid himself, a memory which had penetrated even that splendid armour of indifference in which the man of toil and thought gradually encases himself. The girl's white face, too, and her plaintive eyes, had touched his heart. He felt that this period of suspense was growing almost unendurable!

His secretary entered the room quietly. 'Did you wish me to make any arrangements, sir,' he said, 'for the journey to Scotland?'

Davidson looked at him for a moment as a man without understanding. Then he suddenly remembered that tomorrow was the day on which he was to leave London to join the Lipton's house-party.

'I'm not sure, Ellison,' he said doubtfully. 'I'll let you know in a few minutes.'

Once more he was alone. More impossible, even, than the grim monotony of the days in town seemed the thought of that prim country house, with its well-ordered days, it's fashionable, easy-going crowd of people. He suddenly lost heart as he thought of Lady Catherine and the prosecution of his well-ordered courtship. These things for the moment he felt were impossible. The next day he left London.

Chapter 12

Twenty-four hours later, Davidson was on a wilderness of marshy sands, glittering here and there with the stain of the sea. In the background, a village of red-tiled roofs. Before him, an empty sea. Behind and around, nothing but this stretch of bare, flat country, empty even of the sea until the tide came in. Restless gulls screeched overhead. From inland, a great silence. Here, too, the sea, flowing in upon the level sands, was quiet and noiseless. Davidson felt every nerve of his body at rest. He realized to the full the marvellous joy of solitude. All the strain of those last few days seemed to have fallen away. He looked back upon that passionate of his life as a stranger might look back upon recorded happenings. The tragedy of Brian Haynes, condemned, now in his cell with his head turned toward the door, passing through long hours of torture waiting for the reprieve which might never come. He was almost able to forget that it was he in a measure who was responsible for that episode. He was able, even, to forget the tragic side of Eileen Haynes's visits, - to remember only her gentle, appealing ways, her passionate pleading, her gratitude, tempered still with anxiety, which had triumphed at their last interview over the repugnance which she had at first plainly shown towards him. All these doings and happenings were of another world. Here, trouble and anxiety were like the noxious playthings of a race of children. The sea that rippled in so softly on to the firm sands remained untroubled. The seagulls wheeling above his head in lazy content filled the air with their soothing cries. Everywhere the sunshine lay about the sea-stained places. The green marshes sparkled like emeralds. The wet seaweed, lying about in little heaps, seemed struggling to express new subtleties of colour. Down one of the reaches came a brown-sailed fishing-boat, steered by a man who lay at full length upon the deck, his head upon a coil of rope, one hand only grasping the tiller. A few cows were standing about in the drier part of the marshes, swinging their tails, and moving slowly from one to another of the little plots of herbage. The very smoke from those red-tiled cottages went straight to Heaven, unruffled by even the faintest of breezes. To Davidson it seemed that he had found an idyll of still life, and with a strong instinct of relief, he felt the desire for sleep, so long denied him, creeping over his hot eyes. The drowsiness of the place numbed his senses. The pain ceased. He was content to forget. He threw himself upon the sands, with his back to a sandy knoll covered with weedy green grass, and with the murmur of the sea in his ears, he slept.

Davidson was awakened by a light touch upon his arm. He sat up, and was aware of a girl bending over him.

'I'm sorry to disturb you,' she said, 'but if you sit there for another five minutes, you will be very wet.'

The tide was already within a few feet of them. Davidson realized the position and struggled to his feet. 'It was very kind of you to wake me,' he said. 'I have come down here for a rest, and I suppose I was entering into the programme a little too thoroughly. After London, the sea air is just a little strong.'

She looked at him with interest, and he said the gaze. She was tall - almost as tall as he was himself - slim, with dark eyes, heavy eyebrows, and complexion burnt brown by exposure to all sorts of weathers. She wore plain tweed clothes, in the cut of which his critical eye quickly detected the village tailor. Yet there was something about her appearance which seemed to remove her definitely from behind the pale of rusticity. Her eyes were long, and a little narrow, her eyelids heavy, her mouth had a discontented turn at the corners, and her whole expression was a trifle sullen. He was not in the least prepared for the change in her face when her forehead suddenly relaxed, the corners of her mouth softened, and her lips parted in a dazzling smile.

'You are a Londoner?' she said simply.

'Very much so, I'm afraid.'

'Afraid?' she repeated incredulously.

'Why not?' he said. 'I'm one of the slaves of the world, a man who sits in his office and toils, year in and year out. We're caught in the Golden Web, you see. The time comes,' he continued, 'when we find our way into a little corner of the earth like this, and one realizes the gigantic folly of it.'

'Your point of view is interesting but unconvincing,' she said.

'Why unconvincing?'

'Have you ever thought of the matter from the other point of view?' she said, - 'thought about those poor people, for instance, who have to live in a corner of the world like this, always? All these things, which rest and soothe you here, are beautiful by sheer force of contrast. For a few days - a week or so, perhaps - the contemplation of them would be restful. You would lie about on the sands and in the sunshine and believe that you had found Paradise. And then I think that you would begin to get just a little discontented. The sun doesn't always shine here, you know, and when the sun doesn't shine, all the land is colourless. The sea is grey and ugly, the marshes are flat and dreary, the wind, even in the summer time, is cold.'

He looked at her with interest. She had turned inland, walking very slowly, and he somehow or other found himself by her side, her self-invited companion.

'That is rather a pathetic picture,' he said. 'Anyhow, the solitude remains, and when one has lived with the roar in one's brain, year in and year out, the solitude itself is marvellous.'

'And when one has lived,' she said, 'with the solitude always on one's nerves, lying about one's senses, as though one were the only live thing in a dead and forgotten world, don't you think that one may long for the roar, even as you have come here longing for the solitude?'

'We apparently represent the opposite poles,' he said lightly. 'Tell me, do you live here? I presume, from the feeling with which you speak, that you are a native.'

'I have lived here for nine years,' she said. 'I live in a small house, which you can see just behind the village there. It is very tiny, but very pretty to look at. I have lived there with an aunt who was a farmer's daughter, and is very domestic, and an uncle who was invalided early in life from the Indian Civil Service, and who has done nothing but play golf and fish and study his constitution for the last fifteen years.'

'You don't travel much, then?'

'I have not been out of this county,' she said, 'since I first set foot in it, nine years ago. I had almost given up all hope of ever leaving it, until,' she added, with a little sigh of content, 'a few weeks ago.'

He nodded sympathetically. 'You are going to travel at last, then?' he said.

'I hope so,' she said. 'I have an uncle come home from abroad, who, I believe, is very rich. He wrote to me the day he landed, saying that he was going to send for me to pay him a visit. I'm expecting to hear from him now any day.'

'He is in London?'

'In London!' with a little sigh. 'Fancy,' she went on, turning towards him, 'I have never been in London! Just say that to yourself, and imagine what it means. The biggest town I've ever seen is King's Lynn. Have you ever been to King's Lynn?'

He shook his head. 'I'm afraid not.'

'Then you can't understand,' she said, - 'I couldn't make you understand - what it means to me to think that very soon I'll have a glimpse, at any rate, into the world. If I had met you three weeks ago, probably I'd not have dreamed of waking you up. I'd have let you get wet and then laughed at you. If you had ventured to speak to me, I'd probably have stuck my nose in the air and walked away. You see how mellowing an influence even the possibility of escape is.'

'What a disagreeable young person you must have been!' he said.

She nodded. They were walking side by side now on the top of a tall dyke. On their left-hand side was the creek which flowed into the village from the sea.

'That is precisely my reputation,' she said. 'My aunt detests me. My uncle is always irritable because I can beat him at golf. He is out playing over there now,' she said, with a wave of her hand toward the furthest stretch of the marshes. 'Do you play golf?'

Davidson admitted that he did not.

'You came here, then, only to rest?' she said.

'Only to rest,' he said.

'Where are you staying?'

He turned around and pointed to the square stone tower which stood on the edge of the sea. 'I'm stopping there,' he said, - 'the old Coastguard's Tower they call it, I believe. It is the queerest habitation I have ever been in.'

'You wonderful person!' she said. 'How ever did you get old Pegg and his wife to clear out?'

'I paid them well,' he said. 'At least I didn't do it myself. My man Carter comes from these parts, and he told me about the place and arranged everything. I'm hoping to be able to buy it.'

There was, as he had said from the first, not the slightest reticence about her. She had almost the frankness of a child.

71

'You have a servant?' she said, looking at him with renewed interest. 'Do you mean that he is there with you now?'

Davidson nodded. 'I could scarcely be expected to cook for myself, could I?' he inquired. 'He completes my establishment.'

'I suppose,' she said, 'you are a rich man.'

Davidson shrugged his shoulders. 'Wealth,' he said, 'is a relative thing.'

'Oh! I don't understand those fine sayings!' she said, a little impetuously. 'I only know that to have money is grand, is wonderful. I would give anything in the world to be rich, to have money to spend as I wanted to spend it, and clothes, and jewels, and all the delightful little things of life, to go where I wanted, live as I wished, buy the things I wanted to buy. There's something hideous about being a pauper.'

He looked at her curiously. She was certainly, for all her frankness, a new type. Her frankness was more the frankness of a child than the outspokenness of gaucherie.

'Some day,' he said, 'you may probably have your wish. There is your uncle, for instance.'

She nodded. 'It is my one hope,' she said, 'my one hope. I go to meet the postman every morning. It is three weeks since he wrote and said that he was going to send for me. You don't think that he would change his mind?' she said, turning suddenly towards him with almost tragic intensity.

'Very unlikely, I'd say,' he said. 'Has he any other relatives?'

'None,' she said. 'Even my uncle and aunt with whom I live here are not relatives of his. You see, he was my father's brother. Mr. Brooke was my mother's brother.'

'It is Mr. and Mrs. Brooke you live with?'

She nodded. 'Yes! And my name's Austin,' she said, 'Hannah Austin.'

He stopped short for a minute in the middle of the path. She was walking a little ahead, and missing him in a few moments, turned around. He was standing like a man turned to stone.

'What is the matter?' she said. 'Are you tired, or aren't you well?'

He recovered himself with a little effort. 'It is all right,' he said. 'You know I told you I'd come down here to recoup a little. I get nervous attacks. I was suddenly giddy then.'

She came back. Her face was once more softened in its expression of kindly concern. 'Would you like to take my arm?' she said, a little timidly. 'We are close to the cottage now. Perhaps you would like to come in and sit down. My aunt would be glad to see you.'

'No!' he said. 'Let's rest here for a moment.'

They sat down on the edge of the high, grassy bank. He tortured himself, gazing into her face, trying to find some likeness between her and the murdered man. There was none, he told himself, - none. The name was a common one - one of the commonest. It was ridiculous to connect this girl in any way with the tragedy under whose shadow he had passed. Yet he felt his fingers nervously clutching the bank upon which they were sitting. The seagulls still wheeled above. The tide was flowing softly up into the creek below them. A fishing-boat came gliding by. A lark rose almost from their feet, and was singing just above their heads. Everywhere around was peace and quiet. It was the same land in which he had found content only a few hours ago, yet it seemed to him that already the shadow had come.

It was she who rose first. She shook out her skirts a little reluctantly, and turned toward the village, saying: 'I'm sorry, but I must go. Meals at our house are the one thing more certain than the rising of the sun. We lunch at one, and it's ten minutes to. Do you feel well enough to get back, or will you come on with me?'

'I'll go back,' he said. 'I wonder,' he continued, 'what are you going to do this afternoon?'

She shrugged her shoulders. 'There's nothing,' she said. 'Come out here, I suppose, and pray that I have a letter tomorrow morning.'

'Be unconventional,' he begged. 'Take pity upon an invalid, and come and have tea with me.'

'I'd love to,' she said, 'if I can get away. About half-past four?'

'Yes,' said he. 'I'll be waiting for you.'

'Don't come to meet me,' she begged, - 'not that it matters, of course, only if uncle knew that you were staying there, and that you came from London, and that I had talked to you, he would want to come and call. He is one of those fussy people who like to hear themselves talk, and to make acquaintances. It's all very well for you to shiver,' she added, with a little smile, 'but I have to live with him.'

With a laugh he said: 'I'll hide, until I see you actually before the door. You will come, though?'

'I'll come,' she promised, turning away with a little wave of the hand.

Chapter 13

After all, the element of unconventionality was absent from Davidson's tea-party. About four o'clock, looking landwards from a little sandy knoll just in front of his strange abode, he saw two figures coming along the dyke path. A few minutes later, Hannah Austin and her companion came across the last little strip of shingle, and approached the spot where Davidson was waiting for them.

'My uncle would like to make your acquaintance, Mr. Davidson,' she said.

Davidson held out his hand and welcomed his visitor - a small, fussy-looking little man with a grey moustache. He wore a tweed suit, - very old-fashioned, and of local make, - a flannel collar, and an ill-chosen tie. He shook hands with his host in a perfunctory sort of manner.

'Thought I must just look you up,' he explained, 'living out here. Such a lonely spot, too! You are going to play golf, of course?'

Davidson shook his head. 'I never play,' he said. 'I've come here to rest.'

To rest! The word seemed a strange one to the fussy little man, who was already taking stock of his surroundings. Photographs in silver frames, a pile of books - all new, a gun and fishing-rod, and other such belongings - all, naturally, the best of their sort!

'Well, but you must do something!' Mr. Brooke said. 'You cannot sit here all day and look at the sea, - like the fishermen,' he continued, with a little laugh. 'A very lazy lot - our fishermen, never go out if there's a ripple on the sea.'

Davidson nodded. 'The tides,' he said, 'are rather treacherous, I'd think.'

Carter brought in tea and a great dish of strawberries, at which Mr. Brooke gazed in amazement.

'Strawberries!' he said 'Why, we don't begin to think about them for another six weeks!'

'Is that so?' Davidson said, carelessly. 'I never know anything about seasons. Miss Austin, perhaps you'd like to be mother.'

'You come from London, sir, my niece tells me,' Brooke said.

'From London, yes,' Davidson replied.

'A wonderful place!' Mr. Brooke said, with a sigh. 'Since I retired, I've had to drop out of life altogether.'

'Your health?' Davidson suggested politely.

'My health, and my ridiculously small pension,' Mr. Brooke said. 'I can't make out what the country is coming to. Years ago, pensions were altogether on a different scale.'

'Tell me how you spend your time, Miss Austin?'

'Oh! I do all the obvious things one does, living in such a place,' she said. 'I swim and I fish, I play golf and tennis when I can get any, and I sail a boat when I can borrow one.'

'My niece is seldom satisfied,' Mr. Brooke said sharply.

'Why should I be?' she said. 'You, at least, have had your day. You have seen something of life. I haven't! I dare say, after twenty years away, I might learn to be content.'

'At any rate,' Mr. Brooke said, 'I doubt Mr. Davidson is interested.'

'On the contrary,' Davison said. 'But I thought you told me, Miss Austin, that you were probably leaving us before long.'

'Oh, I hope so!' she replied. 'My uncle was not a man to break his promise, and he did promise. I'm expecting to hear now every day.'

After tea, they wandered out on to the little stretch of sandy shingle which alone separated the cottage from the sea. The girl had walked on a little ahead, and Davidson laid his hand for a moment upon her uncle's shoulder.

'Mr. Brooke,' he said, 'did I understand that the name of your niece's uncle was Austin - the same as her own?'

Mr. Brooke nodded. 'Yes, sir!' he said, - 'Richard Austin. He was her father's brother, you see, - a queer, wandering sort of fish. However, he certainly did write the girl, a few weeks ago, saying that he was back in England, and hoped to realize a large sum of money on some of his investments, and promised to send for her to come up to town. Since then, we have heard nothing from him.'

'Do you read the papers, Mr. Brooke?' Davidson said.

'I read the Times for an hour every afternoon between five and six,' Mr. Brooke admitted. 'I have a special arrangement with Mr. Hewson - the vicar - which enables me to do this, - a special arrangement!' he concluded, with a little gurgle of satisfaction. 'Our vicar, by the bye, Mr. Davidson, is a highly intelligent man. He will doubtless be coming across to see you.'

'I'm here for so short a time,' Davidson said. 'It is very kind of people, but really it is scarcely worth their while to trouble to come to see me. I'm going on to Scotland in a few days. It is only that I was a little run down, and scarcely felt up to a large house-party, that I came here first.'

'You are one of those fortunate people, I see,' Mr. Brooke said, a little enviously, 'who mix in the world.'

Davidson shrugged his shoulders. 'More or less, I suppose,' he admitted. 'But I was asking you whether you read the papers. I did so for an object. I wonder whether you have noticed the details of a very sordid murder that was committed in a London hotel a short time ago.'

'I never read of such things, sir!' Mr. Brooke said. 'They do not interest me. I read the political news and the foreign stuff. Anything that pertains to India, also, naturally claims my attention. I have always contended,' he continued, 'that a golf column in the Times, say twice a week, would be much appreciated. We who study the game from the scientific point of view would like to see the attitude the Times would take on certain matters. For instance, I myself -'

'Pardon my interrupting you, Mr. Brooke,' Davidson said, with his eyes upon the returning figure of the girl, 'but I was speaking about this murder. Curiously enough, the unfortunate man was named Austin, and he had just said from abroad.'

Mr. Brooke slowly opened his mouth. Looking up at his companion blankly, 'You don't for a moment imagine,' he began, 'that there could be any connection between this person and Ruby's uncle?'

'I haven't any idea,' Davidson said, 'but when she mentioned his name, and told me that he had just come back from Africa, and that she had been waiting for a letter which did not come, it certainly occurred to me to be rather in the nature of a coincidence!'

'Have you a paper?' Mr. Brooke said hurriedly.

Davidson shook his head. 'No!' he said. 'But there must be a village library, or some place where the London papers are preserved.'

'There is,' Mr. Brooke said. 'I will hurry back. I will go and read about it at once. Does it say whether the unfortunate man,' he continued, 'was possessed of any means?'

'I do not remember,' Davidson said. 'The object of the murder was supposed to be robbery, but the hotel he was staying at scarcely seemed to be one likely to attract a man of wealth.'

'I'll hurry back at once,' Mr. Brooke said. 'If there is anything in this, I must come and ask your advice.'

'If the thing seems in any way possible,' Davidson said, 'you will have to run up to town and make inquiries.'

Mr. Brooke opened his mouth. 'My dear sir!' he said 'Go to London? But there, there!' he added. 'I forgot! If there is anything in it, the estate would, of course, pay my railway fare. Such a busy week, too, as I have next week,' he added, taking out his memorandum book and glancing at it for a moment. 'I have seven golf matches, - three foursomes and four singles. I scarcely see how I could get away. Ruby,' he called, 'come along, my dear. We must be getting back.'

The girl stifled a yawn. She was beginning to be a bit curious as to why their host had devoted all his attention to her uncle. 'Very well,' she said laconically. 'I'm quite ready. Good-bye, Mr. Davidson!'

'If I may,' he said, 'I will walk a little way with you.'

They crossed the strip of shingle beach together. Afterwards, by necessity, the party became detached. Mr. Brooke walked on ahead. Davidson and the girl followed him, a few yards behind.

'You seem to have found plenty to say to my uncle,' she said curiously.

'If you will spoil an interesting tea-party,' he said, 'by bringing in an elderly male relative, -'

'It wasn't my fault,' she interrupted. 'He would come - insisted upon it - as soon as he knew that I had spoken to you. Your man has been making purchases and sending telegrams in the village, which has made every one curious. People who live in small places are always such snobs.'

He laughed. 'Well, I had to talk to your uncle, anyhow,' he said.

She nodded. 'You know now what I have to put up with,' she said. 'He is a dull, ignorant, pompous little bore. You have probably found that out for yourself by now.'

'You dismiss your relatives a little summarily,' he said.

'I try to speak the truth,' she said. 'I believe in being just to people. If I knew of any good quality that he possessed, I would tell it to you, - but I don't!'

She believed in being just! He looked at her as she walked by his side, stepping along with the delightful freedom of healthy youth, her limbs clearly defined beneath her thin skirt, - for they were facing a land breeze which played havoc, also, with her hair. She walked well, her head a little thrown back. Davidson recognized the graceful lines of her neck and throat. There was something particularly rhythmic about her movements. She was a believer in justice! Well, she looked like that. The mouth, in repose, was a little hard, - the jaw determined. He found himself wondering, with a nervous sort of morbid curiosity, exactly what she would say and do if she had known with whom she was walking, and if Dick Austin had indeed been her uncle! Supposing she knew the whole truth, - knew of that heated interview, knew of Haynes's enterprise, knew of the paper which was still sewn into the dead man's coat! She would scarcely be an easy person to deal with, he thought.

Her uncle had turned round. They had reached the end of the dyke. A little grass-grown footpath led them now to the side of the harbour, beyond which lay the village.

'Mr. Davidson,' he said, - 'Mr. Davidson, I'd like to show you the village schoolroom.'

Davidson nodded. 'I'd be very glad,' he said.

Mr. Brooke turned to his niece. 'Ruby,' he said, 'go home and tell your aunt where we are. I'll be home in half-an-hour, - perhaps five-and-twenty minutes. If there is any message for me from the golf club, the boy can wait till I return. This way, Mr. Davidson, - this way.'

The girl turned away with a little grimace, and waved her hand to Davidson as she disappeared. The two men climbed the village street side by side.

Chapter 14

Mr. Brooke, like most men of his stamp, when brought in touch with larger things than his world knew of, was nervous and helpless. He seemed to throw the whole weight of further action upon this stranger at whose instigation he had started the search.

The reading-room was empty except for these two men. Davidson was sitting in the little bow window, looking down with apparent interest into the narrow, tortuous street. Brooke, with a pile of torn and crumpled newspapers in front of him, was still standing, leaning over the long table in the centre of the room. His search was finished. He had no doubt whatever in his mind. The murdered man was indeed Ruby's uncle!

'Mr. Davidson!' he exclaimed hoarsely.

Davidson turned his head. 'Well?'

'There's no doubt at all about it,' said Mr. Brooke, striking the little pile of papers with the back of his hand. 'It's the man - it's Ruby's uncle! The date of his arrival corresponds, and the hotel is the one from which he wrote to Ruby.'

Davidson nodded. 'I fancied that it must be the same,' he said.

'It is the same,' Mr. Brooke said. 'What are we to do? Something must be done at once!'

'Exactly,' Davidson said. 'Your niece, of course, must claim her inheritance - that is, if the man was really worth anything.'

'Of course! - Of course!' Mr. Brooke said. 'Dear me, what an unfortunate business this all is! I suppose I must go to London with her, and London always upsets me horribly.'

'I'm afraid that you must make up your mind to that,' Davidson said. 'As I said before, if there is anything I can do to help you, I'll be delighted.'

'But you won't be there,' Mr. Brooke said. 'You are going from here to Scotland.'

Davidson hesitated. 'I might,' he said, - 'in fact I think that I certainly should, - go to Scotland by way of London.'

'But we must leave at once!' Mr. Brooke said. 'At least I suppose so.'

Davidson rose to his feet. He had not much sympathy for the frightened little man, whose eyes were continually seeking his as though for help and advice.

'Well,' he said, 'I scarcely see how you can keep away, under the circumstances. You must talk it over with your niece, and let me know what you decide.'

They left the place together. As they stepped out on to the pavement, Mr. Brooke coughed apologetically. 'I suppose,' said he, 'you would consider it necessary for me to tell my niece about this? It will be a shock to her, of course. She had hoped so much from the coming of this uncle, and I'm afraid that she is not particularly contented here.'

'I scarcely see,' Davidson said, 'how you can keep it from her.'

85

'There is no mention of any property,' Mr. Brooke said, - 'none at all. In fact, the papers say that his effects were so small that it seemed difficult to believe that robbery was the motive of the crime. Still, I suppose she must be told.'

Davidson walked down the narrow street, his hands behind his back, his eyes fixed upon the arm of the river below, dotted now with brown-sailed fishing-boats. Here, after all, was a simple way out of the difficulty! The murdered man had no other relatives. In all probability, no one would ever tell the girl. No one would ever claim the possessions of the dead man, whatsoever they might be. Then common sense reasserted itself in his brain, and he stifled the instinct which he had so nearly yielded to.

'She must be told, Mr. Brooke,' he said. 'If you would rather not tell her yourself, I will do so.'

Mr. Brooke shook his head. 'It isn't that,' he said. 'I don't mind telling her. But it's the journey to London, and the excitement, and all that. I hate worry of any sort. It's bad for my health, anyhow.'

They stood upon the little quay, and Davidson hesitated. 'If there is anything further which I can do,' he said, 'come out and look me up. In any case, let me see you before you start for London.'

Mr. Brooke wrung his hand. 'It is very good of you,' he said. 'I'll certainly come out before we start, - most certainly! I can't imagine what Hannah will say. Poor girl! Poor girl!'

Davidson retraced his steps along the high dyke bank to the marshes which surrounded his tower. Once or twice he looked behind, looked toward the low white front of the cottage which the girl had pointed out as her abode. Once he fancied that he saw something moving in the garden, and he stood on the top of the dyke, gazing with a curious interest at the slowly moving speck passing in and out amongst the trees. Then it vanished. He turned and made his way homeward....

Towards sunset, the heat of the day seemed suddenly to increase. A curiously hot wind sprang up from the land, black clouds gathered in the sky, and unusual darkness hung over the land. The air seemed charged with electricity. Every moment it seemed as though the clouds must break and the storm come. The tide came rolling in, no longer with a faint, insistent ripple, but with great powerful waves, throwing their spray far and wide. Davidson left his dinner more than once to stand outside on the little knoll and watch. Every moment he expected to see the banks of black clouds riven with lightning, to hear the far-off muttering across the sea grow nearer and nearer. The whole world seemed to be in a state of suspended animation. The seagulls had ceased their screaming, and had taken shelter in some hidden haunt. A little fleet of fishing-boats had furled their sails. Not a soul was to be seen upon the marshes.

Davidson finished his dinner and sat by the wide-open window, leaning upon his folded arms, looking out at the foam-flecked sea, - foam which seemed to glitter with a clear, white phosphorescence in the failing light. There was something almost theatrical, something breathless, in this pause before the storm! He himself was in an emotional frame of mind. Another page of this tragic had opened before him. The coming of this girl was in itself a catastrophe. She would take possession of the papers belonging to the murdered man, - would show them, probably, to a lawyer. After that, only the worst could happen!

Then, as he sat there, the profound silence was suddenly broken. He heard the crunch of the gravel beneath flying footsteps, the rustle of a skirt, a little half-subdued cry! He looked up in amazement. It was Eileen Haynes who was coming towards him, her hair disordered, her eyes lit with fear, - a strange, half-terrified figure, flying from the storm!

'Miss Haynes!' he exclaimed breathlessly.

Even as he spoke, the clouds were parted at last with a dazzling blaze of forked lightning. The girl gave a little cry and held out her hands. He leaned over, and, as the thunder shook the building, took her into his arms, lifting her over the narrow window-sill into the room.

Chapter 15

Davidson was never quite sure how it had happened. The sudden crash of the storm, the vivid play of the lightning in the darkened room, the curious exultation which any outburst of nature seems to kindle in the forgotten places, had somehow generated a curious excitement - something electrical, incomprehensible, yet felt by both of them. His hands were still about her for a moment after she was in the room. It was perhaps a harmless instinct enough which caused her to draw a little nearer still to him with fear, as the thunder crashed overhead and the ground beneath their feet rocked. Then there happened what he was never able to explain. She was in his arms, her panting breath fell hot upon his cheek, and his lips were pressed to hers, before he even realized what was happening. Her head fell back, her lips seemed to meet his freely, unresistingly. It was one of those moments of madness which seem to be born and die away, without reason, almost without volition. Davidson himself was no Lothario. In his office he had talked kindly with this girl, and it had never occurred to him for a single second even to hold her hand in his. Her comings and goings, except for their association, had left him unmoved. Afterwards, when he tried to think of it, his senses were simply benumbed. Yet the fact remained that she had come into his arms as though she had heard the call of his heart for her that their lips had met with all the effortless certainty of fate.

The thunder ceased. She disengaged herself from his arms with a little cry. Her bosom was still heaving, her cheeks were white almost to ghastliness, with one little patch of brilliant colour where his lips had rested for a moment. She tried to speak, but the words seemed stifled in her throat. He led her to a chair, arranged cushions for her back, and stood over her.

'Is there news?' he said.

'None!' she faltered.

He shook his head. He was completely bewildered. 'How did you find me out?' he said. 'What brings you here at this hour?'

'It is because there is no news,' she cried, speaking with difficulty. 'I cannot rest or sleep. Every moment that passes tears at my heartstrings. Life has become nothing but a living nightmare. Don't be angry with me that I came. I was obliged to do something or I'd have gone mad.'

'I'm not angry,' he said. 'I'm only amazed, I cannot understand -'

'Oh, I found out where you were!' she said. 'I did everything that was mean. I bribed someone to tell me. This morning I saw Brian. I think I came to him at a weak moment. The horror was in his eyes. I shrieked when I saw him. Even now when I think I must shriek. Mr. Davidson, I have come to pray, to beg you to go back. You are very rich. There must be ways of saving him. You have influence with people. Go back and use it. What can you do here in the wilderness? It seems almost as though you had left him to die.'

He stooped down and took her hands once more in his. 'My dear little friend,' he said, 'remember what I told you in my office. Believe me, I'd not have left London if the slightest doubt had remained as to your brother's safety. Never mind how I managed it. You had better not ask; you had better not know. But your brother will be reprieved. It is a certain thing.'

She drew a long breath. Once more her face was at any rate human. The lightning filled the room with a sudden glare. She caught at him with a scream. 'Oh! I'm afraid, I'm afraid!' she moaned.

He passed his arm around her reassuringly. 'You are overwrought,' he said. 'You are almost at the end of your strength.'

He poured out some brandy and water, and made her drink it. Her hand shook so that he had to guide the glass to her lips.

'Listen,' he said, 'you must keep calm or you will be ill, and you will not be able to help your brother. Tell me, have you eaten anything today?'

'I don't remember,' she gasped.

Davidson rang the bell. 'Something to eat,' he ordered, 'for one, as quickly as you can. And some wine - anything will do.'

It was to the man's credit that he received his orders without comment or surprise. Once more they two were alone.

'If you have any faith in me,' Davidson said, 'or any belief, remember what I have told you. Your brother is safe. Tomorrow or the next day the reprieve will be signed.'

'Say it again!' she gasped, clinging to his hand.

'Tomorrow or the next day,' he repeated firmly, 'the reprieve will be signed. There can be no mistake. There will be none.'

'Ah!' she said, half closing her eyes. 'It was to hear you talk like this that I came. I couldn't have borne it alone for another second. Something in my head seemed to be giving way.'

'The storm, too, is terrifying,' he said. 'You were fortunate not to be ten minutes later. Look!'

He led her to the window. Across the marsh was a darkness that was less of the atmosphere than of the falling torrents of rain, - rain that fell in sheets, flung up again from the hard paths of the marshes in a white, fringe-like foam. Seaward, the waves had become breakers. The one white line had become a dozen.

'You would have been drowned,' he said, leading her back to her chair.

'It is good of you,' she said, 'not to be angry. I ought not to have come. I know that. Only I was afraid. In London I'd have gone mad.'

Carter entered with a tray. Davidson stood over her while she ate, walking up and down the room, talking in a disconnected manner of many things. Outside, the storm was passing away. Through the wide-open windows fresh salt air came stealing into the room. Davidson stood looking out for a few minutes, and then turned towards his visitor with an air of perplexity. She met his gaze, and her eyes suddenly filled with tears.

'Oh! I know I have been foolish,' she said. 'I'm here and you don't know what to do with me. Isn't that what you were thinking? I have been very foolish,' she added, with a sudden flood of colour streaming into her cheeks. 'But remember, when I came I was mad. You will remember that?'

'Yes!' he said reassuringly. 'I will remember that.'

There was an awkward silence. Davidson felt that it would have been torture to her if he had alluded to that moment of madness, and yet it was hard altogether to avoid it.

'I'm afraid,' he said, 'that you will have to put up with bachelor quarters to-night. You can have my room here. I have another which will do, but you would find it a little rough.'

She looked at him timidly. 'Couldn't I - get back to the village?'

He led her outside and pointed. The storm, coming with the full tide, had wrought a strange change in the face of the land. Up to the very top of the dykes was a turbulent waste of waters. The tower had been left as though upon an island. Nowhere in sight was any land to be seen.

'You see,' Davidson said to the girl, 'it would not be safe to try and get to the village. The water is up to within a few inches of the dyke, and in the half-darkness one might easily make a false step. From here one cannot quite see, but I'd imagine that the flood is over the village street.'

She turned back toward the little grey stone building. 'If you will let me sleep in your sitting-room, then,' she said timidly. 'I will not turn you out of your room.'

He laughed. 'My dear young lady,' he said, 'if anyone in the world ever needed sleep to-night, it is you. I'm going to send you up to lie down at once. You must promise me, promise faithfully, that you will remember what I have said, that you will say this to yourself: 'The reprieve will come!' It is the truth, mind. Say that to yourself and sleep.'

Then he touched the bell. 'Carter, please make my room as habitable as possible for this young lady. We are on an island, and no one will be able to leave to-night. Put out anything of mine you think may be useful to her.'

She turned towards him impulsively. 'You are very good to me,' she said.

'My dear Miss Haynes, I only wish that it were in my power -'

Then he stopped short. After all, it was not wise to tell her too much. He raised her fingers to his lips, and avoided, with a sudden twinge of self-reproach, the soft invitation of her timidly raised eyes.

'You must sleep well,' he said, as he pointed the way up the stairs. 'Remember, you can take what I have told you as a promise.'

Chapter 16

Dawn and the long waves, remnant of the storm, came gliding in with a slow, lazy motion, and broke noiselessly upon the firm sands. The sky was blue. Of wind there was none at all. Inland, the flood-tide was still high. Only the tops of the dykes were visible. Everywhere the sea had found its way into unexpected places. Little patches of the marsh from which it had just receded shone with a new glory - a green glitter like the sparkle of emeralds. Davidson, who was out early, for his bed had been no more than a sofa, gave a little start of surprise as he opened the door and found Eileen Haynes standing on a little knoll by the side of the flagstaff, looking seaward.

She turned towards him at once with the sound of the opening door. He realized then, more completely than in the dusk of the evening, how great the strain of these last few days had been, - the strain which had driven her into this strange journey. The black rings under her eyes seemed as though traced with a pencil, her cheeks were thinner, and there was something pathetic about the quick, startled look which flashed into her eyes at the sound of Davidson's approaching footsteps.

'I'm afraid,' he said gravely, 'that you have not slept.'

'As much as usual,' she said. 'Tell me, what time do your letters come?'

He looked inland. 'Generally about eight. They may be a little later today.'

She nodded. 'I must go back,' she said vacantly. 'When is there a train?'

It was impossible to ask her to stop, and yet he felt all the pathos of sending her back to face alone the shadow of her terrible anxiety.

'There is no hurry,' he said. 'We will look out the trains after breakfast.'

'Are you - going to stay here?' she said anxiously.

'If I thought,' he said, 'that there was the slightest thing I could do in London which I have not already done, I would go back by the first train this morning, but, indeed, you must remember what I told you last night. The matter is practically settled. In a few days he will know.'

'It is those few days,' she said softly, 'which are so terrible.'

It was hard to try and make use of any conventional phrase of reassurance. Davidson, remembering how intense, how real and startling a thing this tragedy really was, found it hard, impossible, indeed.

'Tell me,' he said, 'do you live absolutely alone?'

'Yes!' she told him. 'There was a cousin who was with me for some time, but she got a situation the other side of London, and had to move. I was in a boarding-house,' she continued, after a moment's hesitation, 'until - this happened. Then all the people - well, they meant to be kind,' she broke off, 'but the woman who kept it thought I had better leave, and I suppose she was right.'

'We will go in to breakfast,' he said, a little abruptly.

Every moment he seemed to realize more completely the pathos of her position. They turned towards the house. Suddenly her fingers fell upon his arm. 'Who is that?' she said, pointing landwards.

Davidson followed her outstretched finger. Riding along the top of one of the dykes, as though unconscious of the sea flowing on either side, came a boy on a bicycle. The bicycle was painted red, and the boy had on a cap whose high peak gave it a semi-official look.

'He is coming here,' Davidson said. 'It may be my letters. Or I think -'

He stopped short. He knew very well that it was a telegram the boy was bringing, but he almost feared to say anything which would bring hope into her face.

'It isn't - it couldn't be a telegram?' she said, a little wistfully.

'It might be,' he admitted. 'I get a good many, of course.'

He told the lie unblushingly. All the time he watched, with an anxiety which seemed incredible, for the coming of the messenger.

'You must remember,' he said, 'that even if this should be a telegram, I really do not expect any news yet.'

She said nothing. She stood with parted lips by his side, and they watched the boy drive his bicycle along the sea-stained bank. Once he skidded, and she gave a little scream.

Davidson laughed at her, surprised to discover something unnatural in the sound.

'Well,' he said, 'we will meet the boy here. I'm afraid you will find a few stock exchange quotations inside the envelope, even if he should be -'

'It is a postman,' she interrupted. 'I can see the bag.'

She clung to his arm. Davidson found himself patting her fragile hand with his strong fingers. He drew her arm through his, and led her a few steps further forward. The boy jumped off his bicycle and opened his wallet, as he approached, with a familiar movement. Davidson took the telegram into his fingers and tore it open. His arm suddenly went round her waist.

'Miss Haynes,' he said, 'be brave and I will tell you some good news. See, you can read it for yourself. The reprieve is signed.'

She suddenly fell a dead weight upon his arm, and almost as quickly she recovered herself. Her closed eyes were opened, she clung to him passionately. 'It is true?' she cried out.

He held the note in front of her face. 'Read,' he said. "Reprieve signed last night. Will be communicated to Haynes this morning. Shackleton.' - That is the name of my solicitor, so there is no possible doubt about it. The matter is ended.'

He turned to the boy, who stood looking on with wooden face. Then he drew a coin from his pocket. 'My young friend,' he said, 'you are in luck. Take that and go home to your breakfast.'

The boy looked at the pound coin and up at Davidson. So far as his features were capable of expression at all, they spoke of stupefaction. Then, as though afraid that Davidson might change his mind, he mounted his bicycle and rode rapidly away.

'It is a relief to you, of course,' Davidson said, trying to speak in as matter-of-fact a tone as possible; 'but this thing was a certainty all the time. I have always tried to make you believe that. Come in now, and let us have some breakfast. You ought to have an appetite.'

She followed him without a word. She seemed, indeed, like a person dreaming, not wholly able to realize the things happening around her, even the moments that passed. Davidson waited upon her at breakfast, and talked in a matter-of-fact way, accepting her monosyllabic answers as natural things, - carrying on a conversation, too, with the man who waited at the sideboard. By degrees, a more natural expression came into her face. When at last the meal was over and Carter had left the room, she burst suddenly into tears. Davidson took her outside and placed her in a chair, sitting by her side on the sands.

'Now,' he said, 'that is all over.'

'When can I go back?' she said suddenly. 'They will let me see Brian. I must go and tell him.'

'He knows, of course,' Davidson replied, 'but naturally he will want to see you. You can leave here in about an hour. I'm not sure - perhaps I may come with you.'

She sat there quietly, absolutely content to lie still and gaze out at the sea. Presently Carter came out with a note, which Davidson silently opened. It was dated from The Cottage.

Dear Mr. Davidson,

My niece knows, and she insists upon going to London at once. We are all very much disturbed. If it is not troubling you too much when you are passing this way, we should be so grateful if you would call in for a minute.

Davidson looked thoughtfully seaward, and his face hardened as he crumpled the note up in his hand. Then he rose to his feet. 'I'm going in to see about the trains for you,' he said.

They stood together on the platform of the nearest railway station, an hour or so later. She laid her arm upon his sleeve.

'Will you stop for a moment, please?' she said. 'I'm afraid I must have seemed ungracious. After all, I ought to be very grateful to you.'

He shook his head. 'No!' he said. 'I ought to have been firmer with your brother when I sent him to this Austin to make terms. It was a desperate enterprise, after all, and I ought to have realized the danger of your brother being tempted to use violence. To me he was nothing more than a unit of humanity, and I took him at his word. If he had brought me the paper I wanted, I was quite prepared to ask him no questions whatever, and he would have been a rich man. I can't help feeling that in a sense I'm responsible for his present position and yours.'

She looked away from him. Her eyes were fixed upon the horizon. She appeared to be steadily thinking the matter out. The wind blew little wisps of fair hair over her face. Her eyes were steadfast, her forehead a little wrinkled. She seemed to be endeavouring to arrive at a conscientious decision.

'No!' she said, after some time, 'I cannot see that you are to blame. I'm sure that it never entered into your head that my brother might be tempted to use violence.'

Davidson looked away with a little frown. In his heart he knew very well that he was not so sure! 'Well,' he said, 'we will let that go. At any rate, my responsibility to you remains. Tell me what I can do? How can I help you?'

She shook her head. 'I'm going back to my work,' she said. 'I need no help.'

'Your work?' he repeated.

She nodded, with a little sigh. 'I'm a typist,' she said. 'You know what that means, - genteel starvation, long hours, grey days. Never mind, I'm almost used to it.'

'You need be a typist no longer unless you choose,' he said. 'Part of what I promised to your brother belongs to you.'

She shook her head. 'Don't speak of it!' she said 'I'd feel that it was blood money.'

'At least let me hear from you sometimes,' he said. 'Don't let me lose sight of you altogether while your brother is unable to help you.'

She hesitated. Then, lifting her eyes to his, 'I don't believe,' she said softly, 'that you would tell me anything that was not true.'

'I don't believe that I'd,' he said.

'Then tell me this,' she said, 'honestly. When you made my brother that offer, when you sent him to deal with this man Austin, can you tell me that you had not an idea in your mind that he might be led on to do something rash?'

Davidson hesitated. He was not a man of over-strict scruples, but he hated lies. Somehow or other, it seemed to him impossible to look at this girl and tell her anything that was not the truth.

'I'm not altogether sure,' he said. 'At the back of my head there was just the idea that your brother was desperate, that he would gain what he wanted, somehow or other.'

She turned away, and walked a little way down the platform. The train was already in the station. She entered a compartment and sat down. 'Thank you,' she said. 'I'm glad that you have told me the truth. Would you mind going away now, please?'

'I'm sorry,' Davidson said simply. 'Remember that I only did what ninety-nine men out of a hundred would have done in my place. I wanted that paper, and your brother begged for just such an enterprise.'

She held out her hands. 'Good-bye!'

Davidson turned away. The girl was damned fool, of course. Yet as he turned and watched the train disappear, he was conscious of a sense of acute depression - none the less acute because it was vague. He turned back to the village, walking with heavy steps. It was as though a new trouble had come into his life.

Chapter 17

Davidson was shown into the Brooke house by an open-mouthed and very country-looking domestic, who regarded him all the time with unaffected curiosity. Mr. Brooke was sitting in an easy-chair, reading the Times. Directly he recognized his visitor he showed signs of nervousness.

'Ah, Mr. Davidson!' he said, rising. 'How do you do, Mr. Davidson?'

Davidson shook hands. His host did not ask him to sit down, nor did he himself resume his seat.

'I looked in,' Davidson explained, 'to know what your niece had decided to do.'

'She has decided to go to London at once,' Mr. Brooke said, - 'at once. It is very inconvenient for all of us. I'm almost sorry that you ever happened to point out the paragraph, especially as there seems to be no property of any sort to be found.'

The door was suddenly opened and Hannah Austin entered. There was a frown which was almost a scowl upon her dark, handsome face. Little Mr. Brooke seemed suddenly to have become a person of no importance.

'Mr. Davidson will excuse me,' he said hurriedly, yet with a marked attempt at stiffness. 'I have to return the Times.'

He left the room. Davidson looked after him with some surprise.

'What is the matter with your uncle?' he said the girl.

'He has just heard,' she said, 'that a young lady from somewhere or other spent the night out at the tower last night.'

Davidson looked at her in amazement. 'And what business is it of his?' he said.

'I don't know,' brusquely. 'As a rule, gentlemen when they're living alone don't have young lady visitors, - not to stay the night, at any rate.'

Davidson laughed. 'The young lady in question,' he said, 'came to see me on a very important matter. If you heard anything of the storm last night, you would understand that it was scarcely possible for anyone to have found her way from the tower to the mainland after the flood-tide was in.'

The girl nodded shortly. 'It's not my business,' she said. 'I'm glad you came. I wanted to ask you something. Who is this man Haynes who killed my uncle?'

Davidson shook his head slowly. 'No one knows very much about him,' he said. 'They were out in South Africa together. It was there, perhaps, that their quarrel, if they had one, started.'

'It says in the Times this morning that he has been reprieved. Why?' she said fiercely. 'Why don't they hang him?'

'Because they came to the conclusion,' he said, 'that there had been a fight, and that it was not a deliberate murder.'

'They ought to have hanged him,' she said. 'It was brutal - hideous!'

'You are going to London, are you not?' he said quietly.

Her eyes flashed. 'Yes!' she said. 'I'm going. I'm afraid it will be too late. All the papers declare that my uncle's possessions were of little value. He has been robbed. I'm sure he has been robbed. His letter told me that he would have plenty of money. He would not write and tell me that if he had nothing.'

'You will be able to find out,' Davidson said, a little coldly.

'I'll find out,' the girl said. 'I'm going to a good lawyer. He wrote as though he had something in his possession which was worth money. It was for that, I'm sure, that this man Haynes tried to kill him. I'll find out all about it when I get there.'

'The man Haynes was arrested on the premises,' Davidson reminded her. 'There was no time for him to have taken anything away, and the room was locked up by the police.'

'I don't care,' she said. 'Oh! Can't you understand what this means to me?' she cried, jumping up from the chair in which she had seated herself a moment or so before. 'I'm starved for life here, starved for the want of it,' she cried. 'I was never meant to live in a place like this - a life like this! It isn't fair. Other girls have clothes and jewels, and men to admire them, and go to theatres, and see the world. Why shouldn't I? I will! I'm going to London to find out what that man killed my uncle for, and I mean never to come back here again.'

The girl was evidently in earnest. Her bosom was heaving, her dark eyes were full of fire. Davidson noticed the firm lines of her mouth, the crisp determination of her speech, and he realized a new danger. This girl was not one to be bribed or put off. Every word she had said she had meant. There was a distinct change in her whole appearance since the last time he had seen her. She was at once handsomer and less attractive. The wistfulness of her few sad speeches to him had passed away. The vague discontent seemed suddenly to have become focussed in a passionate anger against this untoward stroke of fate.

'Well,' Davidson said at length, rising as though about to leave, 'I hope you may discover, after all, that your uncle was a man of property.'

'Why won't you help me?' she said suddenly. 'You could if you would.'

'Could I?' he said. 'I wonder.'

'Of course you could,' she said, coming a little nearer to him. 'I suppose I seem a very ordinary discontented sort of creature to you, but you haven't lived as many years as I have pushing against the walls of a prison. I think I'm one of those persons who would improve a good deal with a little prosperity,' she added, with a sudden smile which transformed her face, a smile which was almost brilliant. 'Why won't you help me?'

'Do you mean that you would like me to go to London for you, and search through your uncle's effects?' Davidson said quietly. 'If you gave me a letter, I suppose I could do that.'

106

'Come with me, then,' she begged. 'I mean to do everything for myself, but there are many little things I'm ignorant about. If you would come with me, I promise you,' she added, looking into his eyes, 'that you would not find me ungrateful.'

'When are you going?' he said.

'Monday morning,' she said.

Davidson walked to the window, and looked out for a moment at the tangled wilderness of cottage flowers, which seemed to have been encouraged to grow there in wild profusion - a brilliant spot of colour, as he remembered very well, from the sea line. In a day or so at most, this girl might, if she realized her position, or if she were properly advised, be in a position to bring ruin upon him. An alliance with her was obviously the very best thing that could happen for him. Yet he felt a certain distrust, a certain unexplained reluctance to accepting her overtures. If she discovered her power, she would drive a hard bargain - he knew that well enough. If she did not discover it -

He turned away and faced her suddenly. 'Yes!' he said, 'I'll help you if I can. We'll go to London together on Monday morning.'

A curious look came into her face. She drew him out of the room. 'Come,' she said, 'I won't ask you to stay to tea, because my aunt thinks that you are a most improper person. I'll walk with you back across the marshes. I want you to tell me what you really think, and I want to show you the one letter I received from my uncle....'

She read the letter to him as they walked side by side on the top of the dyke path, which was high enough now from the receding waste of waters. The air was unusually salt. Great masses of seaweed had been brought in and left by the ebbing tide. The wind had freshened since the morning. She walked on in supreme disregard of her disordered hair and skirts.

'You see,' she said, 'he writes distinctly as one who has, or expects to have, money. Listen! 'I did no particular good out there," she read, "but I have brought something home with me which will mean a fortune of some sort or another. I expect you have had quite enough of your country life, and you won't object to coming and sharing it with me. I'm rather a rough sort, and I have a few vices that your respected uncle Brooke knows all about, but I fancy you will get a better time with me than with that solemn old prig. I'd like to do what I can for you, though we haven't seen much of one another, but your mother was the best sister a man ever had, and for her sake I look upon you as the only relative I've got worth counting."

She looked up at him eagerly. 'Now tell me,' she said, 'would he have written that if he hadn't something - jewels, or estate, or something of that sort, which he knew was going to bring him in money?'

'It doesn't sound so,' Davidson admitted.

She thrust the letter back into her pocket. 'You will help me,' she said, her face glowing, her eyes full of anticipation. 'We will go through his papers carefully. We will find out, somehow or other, what he meant. Oh! It is good to think that

I have only a few more days to eat and to sleep in this ghastly wilderness.'

'You may be disappointed,' he reminded her.

'Never!' she said. 'My uncle was no fool. What he had I'll discover.'

'You may be disappointed,' he continued, 'in the things which wealth itself brings you. You may find life not so very much more wonderful a thing in the city than here in the wilderness.'

'Don't you believe it!' she exclaimed, with a scornful laugh. 'I'm not that sort. I'm not an artist who can sit about here for days and potter about with a paint box, and look at a sunset or a streak of wild lavender, or the shimmering of the yellow sands, as though it were something so marvellous that life itself stood still while they realized it. I like beautiful places and beautiful things, but I hate the impersonality of it all. I want to feel the touch of lace and furs and fine linen, to eat soft food, to listen to music, to ride when I want to, to sleep when I want to, to have friends who admire me, men friends worth speaking to, different from these yokels round here. I suppose I have got it in my blood,' she added, with a little laugh. 'The milk-and-water ways of life don't attract me. I want the big things.'

'Do you know what the big things are?' he said.

'When I have found my way where I mean to find it, I'll know,' she said. 'Here, one might live till one's hair was grey and one's looks had passed, live - if you call it living - and never once see over the wall. When I have come so that I can see over the wall, then I will tell you, if you are still curious, what the big things of life are for me!'

Chapter 18

It was three o'clock in the morning when Davidson softly opened the door of his bedroom in the Hotel Universal, and looked up and down the side corridor. There was no one in sight, no sound of any one passing in the main corridor, a few yards away. For several moments he stood and listened intently. Then he moved a few yards to the left, and stopped opposite another door. He scrutinized the number, - 27. It was the number he sought. He felt in his pocket for the keys which he had collected from various sources. One by one he tried them in the lock. In vain! Not one fitted. He tried the handle of the door softly. There was no doubt about it. The door was securely fastened. He recognized at once the failure of his first attempt, and said to his room. His bed was as yet undisturbed. He had not even changed the tweed travelling suit in which he had journeyed up. It was a fool's errand, after all, he thought, on which he had come. Yet somehow or other, after his conversation with Hannah Austin, after he had realized how thorough her search would indeed be, how convinced she was that somewhere amongst the effects of the dead man lay the secret of wealth, he had realized more completely than ever before the danger in which he stood. Granted, even, that no suspicion of complicity with Haynes attached to him, his financial ruin would be none the less complete if that paper should ever come into the hands of people who understood its worth. Never had the situation seemed so clear, so dangerous, as that night after he had walked home with the girl and turned his face again toward the sea. Something in the very desolation of the marshes seemed to help thought, perhaps by the absence of any distracting object. There was a sense of breadth about the place. As he walked, with only the murmur of the sea in his ears, he saw things clearly. He saw himself in the prime of life, suddenly flung from the place to which he had climbed, flung down to join all those poor millions of strugglers whose first foot has yet to be planted upon the first rung of the great ladder. He was too old to begin at the beginning. There was no place for him down amongst those on whom failure had already placed her mark. He could not have borne it. To be stripped of his riches, his name, the position of which he was without a doubt proud, to suffer the breaking of his engagement, the downfall of all his ambitions, - the very thought of it was intolerable. And in the deep silence of that night, as he listened to the gurgling of the sea below, and the faint movement of the wind across the level land, he realized, with a sudden pain at his heart, the danger in which he stood. In three days the girl would be there. Scotland Yard would send one of its myrmidons with her. She would have free access to all the dead man's belongings. She would take with her a lawyer. Every scrap of paper the man had possessed, every trifling object, would have its value. The Letlakana Mine was world famous. There would be no chance of their overlooking a single document bearing such a name.

Before he had reached his strange dwelling-place he had come to a resolution. Early next morning, stopping only to leave a note telling the girl where to find him when she arrived in London, he was off by the early train. By means of a little diplomacy he had succeeded in gaining a room within a few doors of the one in which Austin had been killed. Only a few feet of wall separated him from the room in which, somewhere or other, was to be found the paper he coveted. Well, his first attempt had been a failure. He knew quite well that the place was paraded by night watchmen, and that any attempt to gain an entrance into the room by orthodox means would result in prompt discovery. There was nothing to be done until the morrow. He threw himself upon the bed and tried to sleep. Waking with the first gleam of daylight, he took off his clothes, bathed, and made a leisurely toilet. Then he rang for the maid.

'Wasn't it upon this floor,' he said, 'that a murder took place lately?'

'In the very next room. We're not allowed to talk about it more than we can help.'

'I'm on the staff of a newspaper,' Davidson said slowly, 'and my people are particularly anxious that I inspect the interior of the room in which that murder was committed. Your people downstairs have absolutely refused to allow me to do anything of the sort. I have taken this room in the hope of being able to get in there. Do you think there is any chance for me?'

'I'd say not, sir,' the maid said. 'The door is locked, and Mr. Hartshorn himself, the manager, has taken the key.'

'There isn't such a thing as a duplicate, I suppose?' Davidson said.

'Not that I know of, sir,' the man said.

'You couldn't suggest any means by which I could enter that room, even if it were an affair of say fifty pounds to you?' Davidson said calmly.

The man started. Fifty pounds was a great deal of money. On the other hand, the fifty pounds would take some earning. 'I'm afraid I can't, sir,' he said. 'There is no duplicate key that I know of, and in any case I dare not run the risk.'

'Fifty pounds is not enough, perhaps,' Davidson said. 'Money is no particular object to me. If you said that you thought you could provide me with the key for a hundred pounds, I would willingly pay it.'

'I'm afraid not, sir,' the man said, turning as though to leave the room.

'Two hundred pounds!' Davidson said.

'It isn't a matter of money, sir,' the man said. 'I daren't do it. I'd be certain to be found out, and I'd be sent away without a character.'

'I will take you into my service,' Davidson said.

The man shook his head. 'Thank you, sir,' he said. 'My character is worth a good deal to me. I think I'll keep out of this, if you don't mind.'

Davidson called him back imperatively. 'Let us understand one another,' he said, drawing something from his pocket. 'Are you going down to the manager to tell him what I have told you?'

The man hesitated. Davidson held out a five-pound note. 'There is no reason for you to do so, you know,' Davidson said, 'just as there is no reason why you should not accept this tip.'

The valet hesitated, and finally accepted the five-pound note which Davidson was holding out.

'I'm sure I don't know why I'd take it, sir,' he said, 'but there is no reason, after all, why I'd say anything of what you have been talking about, downstairs.'

Davidson sat in his chair, waiting. There was a knock at the door and a chambermaid entered, to retire at once in confusion. Davidson looked at her curiously. Something in her figure and her start had seemed familiar to him. He got up and rang the bell. In a moment or two a waiter appeared. He was obviously a German, dark and sallow. He spoke imperfect English, and there was a gleam of cupidity in his eyes which to Davidson seemed hopeful.

'Bring me some tea at once,' he ordered, - 'nothing to eat.'

The man departed, and reappeared in a few minutes.

'Anything else, sir?' he said, after he had set down the tray.

Davidson did not answer him directly. 'By the way,' he said finally, 'wasn't there a murder committed in one of these rooms?'

'It was next door, sir,' the man said.

'The room is locked up?' Davidson said.

'Yes, sir!'

'That is a pity,' Davidson said. 'Do you know who has the key? I'd very much like just to have a look around.'

The waiter shook his head. 'The key is downstairs in Mr. Hartshorn's office, sir, and we have no duplicate here. The police who came, they desired that no one should enter the room until they had removed the effects to Scotland Yard.'

'So I was told downstairs,' Davidson said. 'Do you suppose,' he continued, 'that it would be possible to get hold of a duplicate key? I'd like very much to see the interior of that room - if possible to take a photograph of it for my newspaper. I'm willing to pay.'

The waiter shook his head reluctantly. 'I do not think that there is a duplicate key,' he said, with his eyes fixed upon Davidson's right hand.

'Perhaps you could make inquiries,' Davidson suggested smoothly. 'I want to get a photograph of the inside of the room for my people, if possible. It would be worth quite a great deal of money.'

The man was impressed. 'I will go away and see,' he said slowly.

'Keep this to yourself,' Davidson ordered. 'I don't want it all over the hotel.'

The man made a sign of assent and withdrew. Davidson rang for the chambermaid. Once, twice, three times he rang, without response. Then a middle-aged person came shuffling in, very much out of breath. Davidson gave her some trivial order.

'By the way,' he said, 'are you the chambermaid who waits on this room?'

'No!' she said, with some hesitation. 'The regular chambermaid is down at her breakfast.'

Davidson nodded. 'Will you tell her,' he said, 'that I'd like to see her as soon as she is up? I want to see about some laundry,' he added.

The woman disappeared. Davidson was left alone once more. He unpacked some books, and made himself comfortable in an easy-chair. He was not able even to descend to the smoking-room. Mr. Malcolm Davidson, it was well known, had left town for Scotland. Mr. B. Stocks, who had arrived at the hotel the night before and taken this room, was a person who had particular reasons for not wishing to be seen. Davidson settled himself down to read - a somewhat difficult task. Soon enough, there was a soft tap at the door and the waiter reappeared.

'I beg your pardon, sir,' he said.

'Yes,' Davidson said.

'I have found a key in the service-room which I think would open Number 27.'

Davidson nodded. 'Very well,' he said, 'let me have the use of it to-night, and I will give you fifty pounds.'

The man moistened his lips with his tongue. Fifty pounds was a good sum! But - !

'There is a good deal of risk about it, sir,' the man said slowly, 'and I have to divide with the night-porter, who told me where to find this key.'

'Very well,' Davidson said, 'I will give you twenty pounds each - no more.'

The man placed the key silently in his hands, and Davidson counted out eight five-pound notes.

'If I were you, sir,' he said, 'if you want to be alone in the room and be sure of no one seeing you, I'd use it between four and five tomorrow morning. Everyone is off duty then except the night-porter.'

Davidson nodded. 'By the way,' he said, 'do you know anything about the chambermaid on this floor - the young, slim one?'

The waiter shook his head. 'She has only just come.'

'Do you know her name?' Davidson said.

The man smiled. 'It is always the same,' he said, - 'always Mary.'

'She would not be allowed in 27?' Davidson said. 'She would not be likely to be there to clean it out, or anything of that sort?"

The man shook his head again. 'No one is allowed to enter it,' he said. 'No one has been in but the detectives and lawyers.'

Davidson dismissed the man and settled down once more to his reading. He found it difficult, however, to concentrate his thoughts. The key was on the chair by his side. It was all he could do to restrain himself from stealing down the corridor and commencing his search.

Chapter 19

Davidson remembered afterwards, with a painful exactness, every step which he took in his stockinged feet down the dimly-lit corridor. Only one of the electric lights had been left burning, and that one was encased in a shade of red glass, and was set in the wall facing him. A few seconds ago he had heard Big Ben strike four o'clock. For the last two hours he had sat in his room and waited. Time seemed to have stood still. In that two hours he had seen himself stripped of all his possessions, dishonoured, friendless. He had seen himself married to Lady Catherine, richer and more prosperous than ever, a successful politician, a man on whom the eyes of the world were turned always with respect and approval. Hope and fear had swung in his mind like the movement of a pendulum. All that he needed was that paper! If once he could see it burning into white ashes, or torn into a hundred pieces, he knew that there was nothing in the world strong enough to bar his progress.

Four o'clock at last! At the sound of the hour he had sprung to his feet. Before the echoes of the last stroke had died away he was absolutely committed to his enterprise. For a moment he stood outside the door of his room, which he had left ajar. He looked toward the main corridor and listened intently; there was no sound to be heard. The night watchman - if, indeed, he were making his rounds - was nowhere in that vicinity. In all the great hotel, not a soul seemed to be stirring.

Davidson drew one long breath, and without hesitation stole forward until he stood in front of Number 27. Once more he looked around him. There was only a dimly burning electric light at the end of the corridor. He fitted the key into the lock and turned it. The door swung open. Davidson closed it behind him, turned on the electric light, and gazed around him, his heart beating fast. Within this room, if anywhere, was his salvation!

It was a very ordinary hotel apartment. There was a small single bed, a wardrobe, a table and chest of drawers, a hard, uninviting-looking sofa, and an easy-chair with a stiff back, and armless. Upon the bed were laid out a number of articles of wearing apparel, and upon the floor were two empty cases. Upon the dressing-table were a number of papers, arranged with some appearance of method. The toilet things were still in their places. Everything was arranged in a stiff and precise condition; clearly, official hands had been at work.

Davidson moved toward the dressing-table and started a careful search amongst the papers there. A bill for clothes, a restaurant account, half-a-dozen counterfoils of theatre and tickets, an account for wines and cigars consumed. There was the address of a manicurist, a programme of the National Theatre. Very soon he had come to the end of them. And there was not a single document there of interest or importance.

He turned away toward the clothes which were laid out upon the bed. One by one he lifted them up and laid them down again, until he came to the grey suit which the man Austin had been wearing on the day when he had made his eventful visit to the city. Davidson held up the coat. Nothing. Then he began to realize that this search of his was doomed to end in failure. There was nowhere else to look. He glanced at his watch. Although it seemed to him that he had been in the room for hours, he had indeed been there for barely five minutes.

He moved toward the door, opened it softly, and listened outside in the corridor. There was no sound of anyone stirring, no sign of life or movement anywhere. He said to the room and renewed his search. One by one he lifted up the different articles of clothing and felt in the pockets. His search was rewarded with the discovery of a single halfpenny in an odd waistcoat pocket. He left the clothes alone then and went through the papers once more, with a similar lack of success. Softly he opened all the drawers, ransacked the wardrobe, searched every inch of the room. When at last he desisted, it was because there was nowhere else to look, nothing else to attempt. He stood up in the middle of the room and drew a little breath. He had found nothing, nothing had transpired to compensate in any way for the risk which he had run. Yet there was one consolation. It was scarcely possible that Hannah Austin could be more successful than he. The paper which might make her fortune and ruin him was not here.

Davidson turned at last toward the door. There was no need for him to prolong the risk he ran. He would return to his room, and leave the hotel later in the morning.

He took a few cautious steps toward the door. Suddenly he stopped short and held his breath. Very slowly he turned his head, and listened intently. Someone was stirring in the next room. There was a connecting door, hidden by a curtain, and even as he stood there he heard the handle shake as though it were being turned. He leaned forward and turned out the electric light. Standing there in the darkness he distinctly heard a key inserted in the lock of the hidden door. He heard it softly opened and the curtain pushed back. There was someone else in the room, someone else whom he could not see, someone else who also took an interest in the effects of the murdered man!

There was an interval of several seconds - it seemed minutes - it might well have been hours. Then the stealthy footsteps came towards him. A little stiff rustle of draperies proclaimed the sex of the intruder. Without warning, the electric light flashed out all over the room. The girl would have screamed, but Davidson, who was prepared, leaned forward, and his hand suddenly closed over her mouth. She looked at him with dilated eyes.

'You!' she said 'You!'

'Good God!' he said. 'Eileen Haynes!'

Their mutual surprise was something paralysing. They drew apart and looked at one another as they might have done at ghosts.

'What do you want here?' he said hoarsely.

Was it his fancy, he wondered, or did her lips curl for a moment in something like mockery?

'I came to repay a debt,' she whispered. 'I came to find the paper which you are afraid may fall into someone else's hands. I came to search for it, but it is not here.'

'And I,' Davidson said.

'You have found it, perhaps?' she said

He shook his head. 'It has gone!'

'Perhaps he never had it,' she whispered.

Davidson shook his head. He was being led away by the excitement, the tenseness of the moment, - the unexpectedness of the whole situation. 'He showed it to me,' he said, 'only just before that night.'

'Ah!'

The monosyllable seemed to leave her lips dry. She moistened them with her tongue, and moved a little towards him. There was something in her face which he could not recognize. And then, before further speech was possible, they heard something which, coming so unexpectedly against such a background of silence, terrified them both. An electric bell somewhere close at hand was ringing out its sharp summons into the night.

'What is that?' Davidson said quickly.

'Someone is ringing from one of the numbers opposite,' she said. 'Get back to your room quickly. They have heard us talking. Someone will be in here to search.'

'But you?' he objected.

'I'm safe,' she said. 'I'm on duty on this floor. I have something to do in the next room. Quick!'

He slipped from the door. The little side corridor was as yet empty. For a second or two he listened intently. There were no footsteps as yet audible in the main corridor. In half-a-dozen swift strides he reached the door of his own room, turned the handle, and passed inside. Almost immediately there were footsteps in the corridor outside. The bell of the room opposite was said. Again silence! The seconds grew into minutes, and the minutes passed away. Then his door was suddenly opened from the outside, softly and silently. Eileen Haynes stood there on the threshold of his room, with the handle of the door still in her hand, and to his fancy there was something ominous in the way she looked at him.

'You need search no more,' she said. 'I've found the paper.'

He held out his hand. 'The reward is yours!' he said.

She drew away from him. 'I'll claim it very soon,' she said. 'Ring your bell at seven o'clock, when I'll be on duty, and I will bring it to you. Hush!'

She glided away and closed the door. Davidson drew a long breath. So it was over, then, - over, and he had won!

Chapter 20

Punctually at seven o'clock next morning Davidson rang his bell. Once more the fat old lady entered, with her amiable smile and slow movements.

'Some tea, sir?' she said.

Davidson looked at her for a moment without speaking. 'When does the other chambermaid come on duty?' he said.

'She ought to be on now,' was the answer, 'but she hasn't come. I've just sent the 'boots' up to her room.'

Davidson ordered some hot water and lay still for half-an-hour. Then he rang the bell again. The same woman came.

'Would you like your tea, sir?' she said.

'If you please,' he said.

She was already half-way out of the door before he stopped her.

'You are still on duty, then?' he said.

'The other chambermaid can't be found, sir,' she said. 'Her bed hasn't been slept in, and she doesn't seem to be anywhere about the place.'

Davidson nodded. It was, after all, perhaps the most sensible thing she could do to get clear away! 'Send me my tea at eight o'clock,' he ordered, 'and let me have a bath at once.'

'The valet shall come and tell you when it is ready, sir,' she said.

He passed a tip across to the woman, who accepted it. 'Tell the waiter when he brings the tea to give me my bill,' he said.

In an hour's time Davidson had left the hotel. He had seen nothing more of Eileen Haynes, and on the whole he was disposed to applaud her precaution. He drove at once to his rooms, where Carter was already installed.

'I'll catch the mid-day train to Scotland, Carter,' he said. 'Sleeping-berths. Call the office, and tell them to ring up here at once if a young lady should make any inquiries for me. Perhaps they'd better send her on here.'

He went out and did some shopping. The sun was shining, and a soft west wind blowing. London, which seems to hold its populace longer than any other great city, was gay, almost joyous. He had to elbow his way through crowds as he passed along Piccadilly. The streets and shops were thronged. The sky above was blue. The rare sunshine seemed to make cheerful even this most sombre of cities.

Davidson had the feeling of a man who has escaped from a great danger, - who has been able to throw off a heavy weight. This miserable document of Austin's was as good as in his possession! After all, Brian Haynes was not suffering in vain. The girl should have every penny that he had promised her brother! Her way in life should be made easy! It was a very small price, indeed, to be free from such torture as he had suffered during the last few weeks. He bought presents a little recklessly - presents for Catherine - something, too,

126

for Eileen Haynes. He ordered a large basket of flowers to take with him to Scotland. Then he spoke to his chambers, fully expecting to have some news of Eileen Haynes.

'Any one rung up?' he said.

'No one, sir, of any importance,' was the answer.

'Did you ask the office about Miss Haynes?'

'No young lady at all has inquired for you there, sir.'

Davidson was a little surprised, but after all what did it matter? He travelled up to Scotland with a lighter heart than he had carried for months. Lady Catherine, who met him early in the morning at the small wayside station which was nearest to her father's seat, was amazed at his vivacity.

'I expected to find you a pale, worn-out thing,' she said, as their motor-car climbed the white, stone-bordered road which crossed the heather-covered mountain. 'You don't look as though you needed a change at all.'

'I've found so swift a tonic, you see,' he said, pressing her hand.

She laughed gaily. This was more the man as he had been before the days of their engagement! 'I think it is the smell of the powder,' she said. 'You men are all like schoolboys for your holidays. Father says that the birds are much too wild, and that it will be all even you can do to hit them.'

Davidson smiled. 'There is nothing in the world,' he said, 'which I want to do so much as to lie up there in the heather and close my eyes, and feel the sun and the wind.'

'In other words,' she said, 'you are lazy!'

'Is that laziness?' he said. 'I don't think so.'

'Rest, then,' she said.

'Ah! That is a very different thing!' he replied. 'We all need rest.'

'Especially you,' she said, 'who carry about with you always the memory of some things from which you can never escape.'

He looked at her quickly, but it was obvious that her speech was wholly unpremeditated.

'I often wonder,' she said calmly, 'when I see you in the evenings, how you manage to shake off all your anxieties so easily, for I suppose,' she continued, 'that success, like everything else, carries always its anxieties.'

'Sometimes more than failure,' he said.

'Well,' she continued, 'it doesn't seem possible to associate the word 'failure' with you. Some day you must tell me the whole story of your life. I can scarcely believe that there has ever been a time when you haven't succeeded in anything you undertook.'

He laughed grimly. 'You should have been with me in Africa,' he said, 'after the fighting was over. We expected to go about picking up gold almost on the streets.'

'You were too sanguine,' she laughed.

'It was hard enough work to live,' he said. 'I tried many things, - failures, all of them!'

'Until the Letlakana Mine,' she said.

'Until the Letlakana Mine,' he assented, 'and that, at first, seemed hopeless enough. The mine had been deserted twice. The natives there had a name for it which means the Grave of Dead Hopes!'

They turned into the avenue, and the house was at once visible, standing on the edge of a lake, large and a little bare. The lawns and gardens were brilliant with colour, and the hills on the other side of the water were purple with heather.

'Well, here is all the rest you want,' she said. 'We haven't a neighbour within six miles, and a most harmless lot of guests.'

He drew a long sigh of content. The tragedy, indeed, of the last few weeks seemed to lie far behind in some other world!

Chapter 21

The solicitor hung up his hat, motioned his two visitors to seats, and took his accustomed place in front of his writing-table. 'I'm afraid,' he said, turning toward Mr. Brooke, but in reality addressing his niece, 'that your visit to town has been, in some respects, a disappointment to you, especially bearing in mind the letter which you, my dear young lady, have just shown me. Still, there is no getting away from facts. We have carefully examined every paper and every portion of the personal belongings of the deceased, and I'm afraid we must come to the decision that there is nothing in those effects worth taking away.'

'It certainly seems not,' Mr. Brooke assented. 'I must say that from the first I have discouraged my niece in her expectations. I never knew Austin, but everyone spoke of him as being a shiftless and impossible sort of person.'

The lawyer nodded. 'From the state of his effects,' he said, 'that seems very possible, and yet one cannot help wondering what it was that he had in his mind when he wrote to your niece, - what it was, too, that induced him to take rooms in a hotel like the Universal.'

Hannah Austin rose slowly to her feet. She came to the table before which the solicitor was seated, and she looked down at him with blazing eyes. 'Can't you see, you two,' she exclaimed, - 'can't you understand that the man has been robbed of something? He would never have written me in that strain if he had not believed that he possessed something which was at any rate worth money, and a great deal of money. He would never, with only twenty pounds in his pocket, have gone to a hotel like the Universal, drunk champagne there, and lived as though his means were unlimited. These things are ridiculous!'

'But, my dear young lady,' the lawyer started, -

'Can't you see the truth?' she said 'My uncle was murdered. Why? What was the motive? Robbery! Do you think that it was for the sake of the twenty pounds or so that he had on him, and which were found untouched? The man Haynes was in South Africa with my uncle, - he knew his business. It was no ordinary quarrel, this. I tell you that Haynes robbed my uncle of something - I don't know what - but something which was the backbone of this letter!' she exclaimed, dashing it upon the table, - 'something which justified him in staying at the Universal, something which must be found!'

The lawyer nodded. 'That point of view,' he admitted, 'has occurred to me, I must confess. And yet, you must remember that the man Haynes was arrested upon the premises. He had nothing with him which could by any chance have belonged to the dead man.'

The girl stamped her foot impatiently. 'Have you read the evidence at the trial?' she said. 'It is very clear that this man Haynes was no fool. Whatever he wanted from my uncle, he secured and disposed of before he was arrested. The last thing he would do would be to carry about with him on his person anything which he had taken from my uncle.'

'What you suggest may be possible, of course,' the lawyer said, 'but, unfortunately, we have not the slightest indication of it. The man Haynes was not seen to speak to anyone in the hotel, and it is known that he did not leave it after the quarrel until his arrest.'

'And you are content to leave it like that?' the girl said.

The lawyer shrugged his shoulders. 'It is not that we are content,' he said, a little stiffly, 'but there certainly seems to be no cause for any further action.'

The girl turned to Mr. Brooke. 'We had better go,' she said abruptly. 'There is nothing to be gained by staying here.'

The solicitor accompanied them to the door. 'Miss Austin,' he said, 'I can sympathize with your disappointment, but I do beg of you not to go looking for a mare's nest. It is disappointing, of course, to find that your uncle was practically a pauper, especially after that letter of his, but, on the other hand, men in his position, I'm afraid, are proverbially given to exaggeration.'

'Thank you,' the girl said sharply, 'I think that we'll not talk about this any more.'

Mr. Brooke and his niece walked slowly up a little side street which led into the Strand. The former, who was sharing to some extent his niece's disappointment, found compensation in the thought of a speedy return.

'I'm afraid, Ruby,' he said, 'that you are very much disappointed, and it seems to me that we have wasted our railway fares to London. It can't be helped. We may as well make the best of it and get back at once. I can see no reason why we should not catch the three o'clock train. I'll be able to play my match, then, with Colonel Fawcett tomorrow morning.'

'You can go and play your match if you want to,' the girl said. 'I'm going to stay in London.'

'To stay in London?' Mr. Brooke repeated.

'I mean it,' the girl said. 'I don't mean to be robbed. I mean to stay here and find out why this man Haynes quarrelled with my uncle, and what my uncle meant when he wrote to me about a fortune. You go back, if you like,' she continued. 'Give me five pounds to stay here with, and I'll come back when I've found out the truth.'

Mr. Brooke was aghast. He looked at his niece with wide-open eyes. What had come to her that she should speak of such a sum as five pounds almost carelessly!

'I'll do nothing of the sort,' he said decidedly, 'nor shall I allow you to stay up here alone - a most improper proceeding, I'd call it, - quite unheard of. We will go back to the hotel, pay our bill, have a little lunch at an A B C shop, and catch the three o'clock train home.'

'If you won't let me have the five pounds,' she said, 'all right. Good-bye!'

She turned abruptly away, and before his astonished eyes plunged into the stream of traffic, making for the other side of the street. He followed her as soon as he saw a safe opening, and found her on the point of entering a small restaurant.

'My dear Ruby,' he exclaimed sharply, 'you are mad! How dared you leave me like that?'

She shrugged her shoulders. 'I have been mad,' she said, 'to live that awful life for these last few years. I've had enough of it, uncle. I'm here, and I'm going to stay here. If I can't succeed in what I'm going to undertake, I'll try and find some work.'

Mr. Brooke gasped. It was a wholly unexpected revolt. 'You mean to say that you don't want to come back?'

'Never, if I can help it!' the girl said. 'I hate the place. I hate the life. I'm tired, sick to death of it all!' she cried passionately, 'and I would as soon come up here and live for a week or two, and then throw myself into the Thames, as go on with it any longer. If you won't let me have the five pounds,' she continued, 'I have enough jewellery with me to fetch about that. The money would only mean a week or two longer.'

'But where would you live?' he said 'What would you do?'

'That is my affair,' she said simply. 'First of all, though, I'd go to Mr. Davidson, and I'd ask him to help me. Any man of common sense would agree with me at once in believing that my uncle was robbed.'

'But your aunt?' Mr. Brooke exclaimed weakly.

'My aunt can get on very well without me,' the girl said.

Mr. Brooke felt that a situation had arisen with which he was unable to cope. The only thing that occurred to him to do was to temporize. 'You will have to come back to the hotel,' he said, 'to get your luggage. We will talk it over on the way there.'

'Just as you please,' the girl said carelessly, 'only so far as I'm concerned, there is nothing to talk over.'

Mr. Brooke hailed a 'bus which deposited them presently within a few yards of the semi-private hotel in Montague Street at which they were staying. It was one of those establishments which, from being a small boarding-house, had blossomed out into a hotel, with all the outward signs of its more prosperous rivals. There was an entrance hall, a reception office, and two long-limbed giants in light blue livery, who spoke every language except their own. The people who frequented it were either Americans, or people from the isolated country places, such as Mr. Brooke and his niece.

'I'm not going to talk anything over until I have had some lunch,' the girl said. 'We need not go out. It is only a few quid each here. You can afford that, especially as you are probably going to be rid of me forever.'

Mr. Brooke frowned. 'We will lunch here if you prefer it,' he said. 'I'm not aware that I have hesitated at anything on the score of expense.'

The girl laughed. There was a note in her mirth which was strange to Mr. Brooke. He relinquished his well-worn silk hat to a boy in buttons, straightened his old-fashioned tie before a passing mirror, and led the girl into the dining-room. The size of the apartment, the number of the waiters, the indefinable sense of being in a great city, which had oppressed him since the train had rolled into the terminus on his arrival, once more had its effect upon him. He felt sure that his niece understood nothing of what she was talking

135

about. He drank bottled beer with his lunch, and soon summoned up courage to reopen the matter.

'It was a very good idea of yours, my dear Ruby,' he said, 'to lunch here. I'm sure that for the money it is a most excellent meal.'

She gave vent to a little interjection which might have meant anything. If he had not been so sure that she was unused to such magnificence, he would have believed that it was intended to indicate a certain amount of contempt at her entertainment.

'And now,' Mr. Brooke continued, 'let me speak to you seriously.'

The suggestion that there had been anything of mirth from which Mr. Brooke desired to lead the way appealed to the girl's sense of humour. Her lips parted, and the sullen discontent of her face was for a moment lightened.

'Very well,' she said, 'let us be serious. Go on. Tell me what you have to say.'

'What I want to put before you is briefly this,' he said. 'You do not understand the impossibility of a young girl barely twenty years old, with your' - he coughed a little - 'personal attractions, being left alone in London. Of course, it is difficult for me to explain to you exactly what I mean.'

'You needn't,' the girl interrupted contemptuously. 'Do you think that I'm a fool? I know all about those risks which people speak about with bated breath, and I'd like you to know that I'm quite able to take care of myself. I'm not afraid, so I do not know why anyone need be afraid for me.'

Mr. Brooke looked at her and wondered where amongst the wastes and wind-swept places of his lonely home had the girl acquired the knowledge which she alluded to so scornfully, - had she learned, too, he reflected, to carry herself, as she had done since their arrival, with an ease and assurance which he had tried in vain to emulate. He realized at that moment that all further argument would be wasted. Nevertheless, he continued to ease his conscience.

'You may know a good deal,' he said, 'or think you do, - girls nowadays read and talk of most surprising things, - but London is not a safe place for a young girl, whatever you may say, especially a young girl without enough money to live on.'

'I suppose,' she said, laughing at him openly, 'it's a safe place. Well, I have tried it for a good many years, and I have had enough. You needn't be afraid,' she continued, 'that I'll return in the guise of a prodigal daughter. If I don't succeed in tracing Richard Austin's fortune, I'll find something else to do. If you will give me the five pounds I ask for, it will make things easier. If not, I'll get on without it.'

He felt that he was being weak. Even his conscience told him that greater firmness was necessary. And yet he recognized something in the girl's demeanour which assured him absolutely that any protests were hopeless. There was a hidden strength there, shared by neither her aunt nor himself, - something which kept her apart from them, - which made him half believe, in spite of himself, that what she set herself to do she would accomplish.

'At least,' he said, 'we must know where you are going to live.'

'There is no need for you to stay in London,' she said, 'while I look about for a room. I know exactly the sort of place I'm going to take. I'm going out in the Tube to one of the suburbs, where a bedroom is not very expensive, and I'll take my meals out. It will cost me very little to live, and five pounds will go quite a long way. By the time it is spent, I think that I'll have discovered something. I will not write you for any more money, I promise.'

Mr. Brooke sighed. 'I suppose you must have your own way,' he said. 'I don't know what your aunt will say.'

She laughed. They had finished their luncheon and had risen from the table. 'Enough about my aunt,' she said. 'She will have all the anxiety of her preserves upon her mind directly, and I think she will be glad not to be bothered with me. You catch your three o'clock train, and play your golf match tomorrow.'

'I suppose I may as well,' he said weakly, 'although I never can putt after a railway journey.'

'Go and try, anyhow,' she said. 'We will say good-bye to one another here, if you don't mind. The porter will take care of my luggage until I have taken my room.'

'I suppose if I were to stay up with you for a few days,' he began, -

'Please, uncle, don't!' she began firmly. 'It isn't any use. You have been kind to me in your way, but the life there is horrible to me. I have made up my mind to have no more of it. You've done your best for me, you can't do more. Good-bye! There is your bag, and you haven't too much time to catch the three o'clock train. Take the first turn to the left from here, and book to King's Cross by the Tube. Good-bye!'

Mr. Brooke picked up his bag and departed without any further protest. The girl stood upon the steps and watched him, and as she watched, some of the darkness seemed to pass away from her face. He disappeared around the corner. She was alone - free, at any rate! She drew a long breath, and the dull streets and grey sky seemed suddenly to have become like the walls and canopy of a new paradise.

Chapter 22

At about quarter past ten in the morning, a man, still young, but deathly pale, with hollow cheeks and receding eyes, stood on the edge of the pavement outside a great and gloomy-looking building. A nail-studded door had just been opened and closed to let him pass. The attendant, who wore prison livery, leaned forward curiously to look at him as he walked out with uncertain footsteps. The prison doctor stood by his side and called a cab.

'You are sure,' he said, 'that you have somewhere to go to, Haynes?'

'Quite sure, sir,' the man said.

'Keep your courage up, my man,' added the doctor. 'If your friends can afford it, go down to the South at once. You will find it easier there. There's your cab. You have some money, have you not?'

'Plenty, thank you, doctor,' Haynes said. 'You've been kind to me, sir,' he added. 'Thank you!'

'There wasn't much I could do,' the doctor said, helping him into the cab, 'except to get you out of this hole. Make the most of your time now. Good luck to you!'

The cab rolled off. Haynes, after the first few minutes' exhaustion, due to his unaccustomed preparations, leaned forward on the seat, looking out with hungry, wistful eyes upon the world which he had scarcely hoped to see again. Very soon the full flood of London traffic was flowing past him, the streams of men and women jostling one another upon the pavements, the long, tangled thread of moving vehicles, taximeter cabs, hansoms, and wagons. The sun was shining, the faces of the people seemed to him accustomed to the white, hopeless countenances of the men he had passed in his daily exercises and in the prison infirmary, unusually buoyant and cheerful. It was a glad world, this, into which he had come, a world which he was so soon to leave. It was hard to think he was free only that he might crawl away into some corner where he could die.

The cab stopped at last before a block of offices in a by-street of the city. Haynes reluctantly alighted, and crossing the pavement entered the building. He passed through a swing door to a desk. A small boy poked his head out of an inquiry office.

'Can you tell me if Miss Haynes is employed here?' Haynes said.

'Yes, but you can't see her,' the small boy said. 'She's in with the boss.'

Haynes hesitated. 'Perhaps you will kindly tell her when she's finished that her brother is here, and would like to speak to her.'

The office-boy withdrew his head, but he seemed uncertain. Haynes seated himself upon a hard bench set against the wall. On a small round table in front of him were pens and paper and a copy of the trade journal. Haynes turned over its pages listlessly for a moment or two, and then set himself down to wait. It was quite half-an-hour before a door in front of him opened, and Eileen Haynes appeared. She looked at her brother in blank astonishment. She was paler than ever, there were dark rings under her dilated eyes. She looked at him as one looks upon some strange monstrosity.

'Brian!' she said. 'It can't be you! And yet - Brian!'

'It is I,' he said.

'Free?' she cried.

He laughed, a little bitterly. 'They have let me out to die,' he said. 'The doctor today signed a certificate that I have no reasonable chance of living longer than another month, so here I am, free, Eileen, if you like to call it freedom.'

She came and sat on the bench by his side. At that moment it was hard to say, from their appearance, which of the two seemed the nearer death.

'When were you released?' she said.

'Half-an-hour ago,' he said. 'I came straight here. I wondered whether you could get a month's vacation, and come with me somewhere south. We have enough money for a little time.'

'If they will not let me go,' she said, 'I will leave. That is simple enough. We have enough money, Brian. We will go this afternoon.'

He shook his head. 'First,' he said, 'I must see - I must see -'

'Whom?' she said.

'A friend,' he said, 'someone who may be inclined to do something for me, - not for myself,' he added hastily, - 'that, of course, is ridiculous - but it is of you I'm thinking, of you after I'm gone.'

'I'll be all right, Brian,' she said. 'We have several hundred pounds left, you know.'

'It is not enough,' he said firmly. 'Eileen, will you go on an errand for me?'

'Where to?' she said, with a sudden sinking of her heart.

'To a man whose address I will give you, - a rich man, a great man. I think that he will be willing to do something for us. His name is Malcolm Davidson. I will write his address down for you.'

'Mr. Davidson!' she repeated. 'I have been before to see him, Brian. I went before your reprieve came.'

'Of course,' he said. 'I had forgotten. Well, I want you to go up to him now. I want to see him, but I do not want to go to his offices. Where do you live, Eileen?'

'I can't take you there.'

'Then we must go to a hotel,' he said. 'It seems a mockery to buy clothes, but there are one or two things I must have. Tomorrow we will go somewhere south.'

She glanced at the clock. 'I will see whether I can get away now,' she said.

She disappeared, and came out again in a few minutes with her hat on. 'Come,' she said.

He led her to the cab outside. 'We'll drive to a hotel,' he said. 'When we have taken some rooms, you can go and see Mr. Davidson. I think that he will come to me if you will tell him that I'm free, that I have only three weeks to live, and that I'd like to see him.'

143

'Very well,' she said.

They stepped into the cab. 'Tell him to drive to one of the large hotels,' Haynes said, - 'any except the Universal.'

She shuddered as she gave the order. She, too, had her memories of the Universal, of which he knew nothing. Slowly they made their way westwards. The girl held his hand in hers.

'It is good to see you again, Brian,' she said.

'It is good to be here again,' he said, 'to be out in the world, even though it be to die. I suppose the authorities have really been kind to me. It is as much as anyone could expect. And yet, Eileen, I'd like you to remember this always. The quarrel between Austin and myself was of his seeking - not mine. The blow of which he died was struck purely in self-defence. I could box and he couldn't, or he would have half killed me that night.'

'I know,' she said breathlessly. 'Don't talk of it.'

He went on, as though not hearing her. 'He came at me with both hands clenched, and I hit him under the chin. I had to, or he would have killed me if he could. He was a strong man, and he had been drinking until he was half mad. It was not my fault, Eileen.'

'Oh, I know that!' she said. 'Try and forget it now. It was a wicked, wicked accident.'

'Life has been wicked enough for you and me lately,' he said, sighing. 'You are worn to a shadow, Eileen. I suppose it is this wretched typing, day by day. We must put an end to it.'

She shook her head. 'I must earn a living, dear,' she said. 'But don't bother about me. I'll be all right. See, he has stopped. This must be - yes, it is the Grand Hotel. Will that do?'

He nodded. 'Quite well,' he said.

He paid the taxi driver, and making some excuse at the office about luggage to come, took rooms. Then he put Eileen into a taxi, and wrote down for her Davidson's address, which she already knew.

'Bring him back with you if you can,' he begged. 'Bring him back here. I'll be waiting in the reading-room, just round the corner there to the right.'

She hesitated. 'You look so faint, Brian,' she said. 'I'm not sure whether I ought to leave you.'

'I'm going to have some brandy and milk,' he said. 'I'm going to sit down and have it there in that corner. I'll wait till you come. You will know where to look for me. Hurry, dear, please. I'll know no peace until I have seen Davidson.'

Chapter 23

Davidson sat at his desk, immersed once more in the affairs of his business. His cheeks were bronzed with the sun. His eyes were clear and bright. All traces of the turmoil and disturbance of those few nervous weeks seemed to have passed away. One thing only occasionally disturbed him - the non-appearance of Eileen Haynes. Since those few seconds of tremulous excitement when they had stood face to face in the darkened room of the hotel, he had neither seen nor heard from her. He could understand her having left the hotel hurriedly. He could have understood her keeping away for a day or two. But a whole month had passed, and she had taken no steps whatever to communicate with him. He had left exact instructions as to what was to be done should she come to the office while he was in Scotland. He had had the whole of his private letters forwarded, lest by chance a word from her should fail to reach him. There was something a little ominous in this absolute silence, something which troubled him occasionally, which set him thinking, wondering, whether under that still, quiet demeanour there might be qualities of which he had taken no account, - whether indeed she, too, were not a schemer who meant to make the most of this opportunity which chance had thrown in her way.

A clerk entered and stood at his side. 'A young lady is here to see you, sir,' he announced, - 'Miss Haynes.'

'Miss Haynes,' Davidson repeated mechanically.

'Yes, sir!' the clerk said. 'We have instructions outside to let you know if she called at any time.'

Davidson leaned back in his chair. With a few quick words he dismissed his secretary from the immediate business in hand. 'You may show Miss Haynes in,' he said.

A moment or two later she entered. Davidson watched her with a new curiosity as he rose to his feet. She was as quietly dressed as usual, as pale, and her eyes, except for one upward glance, seemed always to be seeking the carpet. There was something curiously negative about her appearance, - something, it seemed to him, almost wilfully so. The rich brown hair, which had flashed almost to golden in the morning sunlight, was drawn up and concealed, as though the owner's sole object was that it might escape attention. Her clothes were not unbecoming, but they were the quietest of their sort. Her eyes, which should have been beautiful, were so perpetually veiled and hidden that their quality was lost. Both physically and in her reticent speech she appealed to him more than ever that morning as a woman whose desire seemed to be to creep through life unnoticed.

'At last!' he said, holding out his hand pleasantly. 'I have been expecting to see you for some time, Miss Haynes.'

'You have been expecting to see me?' she repeated, raising her eyes to his. 'How strange!'

'Why strange?' he said, glancing around the room, and lowering his voice a little. 'Don't you remember at our last meeting you promised to bring my tea a few hours later? Since then, I have not even seen you, nor have you sent me a line.'

She raised her eyes again and looked at him. They were very beautiful eyes, but he did not understand the somewhat blank expression which shone out of them. 'I do not understand you,' she said quietly.

Davidson would have been irritated, but something in her manner struck him as so strange that his feeling turned to one of bewilderment. 'Come,' he said, 'you are not going to suggest that I have been dreaming, or that you have had one of these fashionable lapses of memory? You remember meeting me in that room in the Universal Hotel?'

Without change of countenance or expression she said, 'I have never been in the Universal Hotel in my life!'

Davidson looked at her, his lips a little parted, and as he looked his feeling of bewilderment grew. 'My dear young lady,' he protested, 'do you mean to tell me -'

'You have been mistaking me for someone else, I think,' she said calmly. 'There are so many people about who are like me. We will not talk of this just now, if you do not mind. I have come to you from my brother.'

'Well?' Davidson said.

'My brother is free,' she went on. 'He was released at nine o'clock this morning. The doctor at the prison signed a certificate that he has only a month or so to live. He is free on the understanding that he goes away to some quiet place. He came to me an hour ago. It is at his wish that I'm here.'

'Go on,' Davidson rapped out.

'He wishes to see you,' she said. 'That is all. He does not think that there is any risk about it, under the circumstances. We are staying for the night at the Grand Hotel. Tomorrow we shall go down to Devonshire or Cornwall. He will be glad if you will come and see him as soon as possible.'

'I will come,' Davidson said, 'but first, Miss Haynes, I must have an understanding with you.'

'An understanding with me?' she repeated slowly.

'Naturally,' he said. 'I want to know, first of all, whether you are my friend or my enemy, - whether, in short, you mean to play the blackmailer, or whether you mean to return to me that document which you abstracted from amongst Austin's effects.'

She drew a little sigh. 'I'm quite sure now, Mr. Davidson,' she said, 'that you are mistaking me for someone else. I do not know what you are talking about.'

Davidson was silent for several moments. He was feeling nervous and disturbed. There was something uncanny about this quiet, persistent denial, - the still face, the steadfast, beautiful eyes, which seemed yet like unlit fires devoid of sympathy or apprehension.

'I scarcely know,' Davidson said, 'how we are to continue this discussion. For some reason or other, you are sitting there within a few feet of me and denying something which we both know to be the truth. You have a motive, I suppose, but whatever that motive may be, you cannot imperil it by speaking openly here. We are absolutely alone. There is not a soul within hearing. You and I both know, Miss Haynes, that you hold that paper to obtain which your brother risked his life and met with such misfortune. It would be his wish, I know, that you should give it to me. The terms I offered him for its recovery were surely liberal. If you think otherwise, tell me your price. We are alone. You are not giving yourself away. Tell me your price!'

'I have no price, Mr. Davidson,' she said, 'because I have no paper. I'm not a thief, nor have I stolen anything from anybody. All that you say is strange to me. My brother is waiting, and he is very ill. Will you come with me now, or will you follow as soon as you can?'

Davidson leaned back in his chair and laughed. It was not altogether a natural laugh, but it was the only relief he could find from his overwrought feelings. 'What sort of a game you and I are going to play, Miss Haynes, I cannot imagine,' he said. 'I have made the first and the obvious move, and you have said your opening. We must let it go at that, I suppose. When you are disposed to talk common sense, I and my cheque-book will be glad to listen to you. In the meantime, let me beg of you one thing, and that is, keep that paper in some safe place!'

She rose to her feet with a little sigh. 'You are mistaking me for someone else, Mr. Davidson,' she said.

He crossed the room and fetched his hat and gloves from a cupboard. He glanced into a looking-glass for a moment to straighten his tie, and met the girl's eyes fixed upon him. He stood quite still, watching. She was looking at him, at his back, as he stood there. There was expression in her face at last, an expression which puzzled him, which he failed altogether to understand. He stood quite still, with his fingers still upon the sailor knot of his tie. As though she realized the possibilities of the mirror, she suddenly turned around. When he came towards her, the mask, if it was a mask, was there once more.

'If you will come with me,' said he, 'I'd be glad to go and see your brother.'

They passed through the offices side by side. Many curious eyes followed them. Davidson paused at one or two of the desks to leave a few parting instructions. Then he handed the girl into the electric taxi which was waiting at the door.

'The Grand Hotel,' he told the man.

He got in and seated himself by her side. 'Miss Haynes,' he said, 'you are beginning to interest me exceedingly.'

'I'm sure that you cannot be in earnest,' she said, without turning her head. 'I'm a most uninteresting person, living a most uninteresting life.'

'I think you said that you were a secretary.' 'I am. I've been there for three years.'

He deliberately leaned forward to look into her face. The memory of that moment when he had held her in his arms, the breaking of the storm, the thrill, the wonderful, unanalysed excitement which seemed to play about them like the lightning which was soon to flash across the sea and land, came back to him. He looked deliberately into her face, - still as the grave, - at the large eyes, which were listlessly fixed upon the streaming people.

'You are the most amazing person!' he said softly. 'Perhaps it was not you who came to me with the storm, who tapped at my window, who stood there like the daughter of the storm itself, who -'

'It was me,' she said. 'You know that very well, Mr. Davidson. Neither have I forgotten it. But I think that you should not remind me just now of that.'

Of course she was right, but Davidson felt a little unhinged. Her invulnerability was maddening. 'Perhaps not,' he said. 'Perhaps I have no right to remind you of that night, of the time when you crept in from the storm, crept into my arms.'

She turned her head slightly away, as though interested in the passing throng. No flush of colour tinged her cheeks. Her straight, firm lips never trembled. He tried to take her hand, - small it was, and encased in old, neatly-mended gloves. She drew it quietly but firmly away. She remained silent.

'Perhaps I have no right,' he continued, 'to remind you of these things, but neither have you the right to deny our later meeting. You are playing some sort of a game with me,' he continued, a little roughly, 'and your methods, whatever they may be, include a lie. Therefore, I myself take license.'

'If you have quite finished, Mr. Davidson,' she said, 'I'd be glad. My visit to you, and all the circumstances connected with it, is one of the things which I wish to forget.'

'To relegate to the same place in your memory,' he said, 'as your brief essay in the rôle of a chambermaid.'

She leaned out of the window. 'Here we are,' she said. 'I'm anxious about my brother. Please hurry.'

Chapter 24

Haynes sat still in his corner, and although the hotel could not be called fashionable - perhaps, in these later days, scarcely luxurious - the little ebb and flow of life upon which he looked seemed tinged with a peculiar bitterness. His hollow eyes followed each group of these men and women, so full of vivacity, of happiness, of affairs. The envy in his heart was like a real and passionate thing. It was an envy scarcely founded upon comparisons. For them was life, - for him was none! In front of him always was that ghastly, unchanging verdict: a month - two at the most - thirty days of ill-health, of suffering, of weakness, and after that - what? He caught his breath with a little shudder, and calling a passing waiter, ordered some brandy. He looked around and longed to find someone to speak to, someone to occupy his attention for a single moment, to stop the flow of gruesome fancies which seemed always biting their way into his brain. He had faced death readily enough in those old days, when Davidson and he had ridden side by side, and the bullets had whizzed around them like rain, and the dead men lay in heaps. But this was different! The blood ran warm in their veins then, their hearts were strong. He had no strength now to battle with these fancies, no strength to do anything but cower before the slowly coming, grisly shadow of his fate. He looked continually at the door, longing always for the return of his sister and the coming of Davidson. Even the prison hospital was better than this.

A girl passed by, young and beautiful, carrying in her arms a little dog. She threw a compassionate glance at Haynes, and he felt the sweat break out upon his forehead. It was too awful, this! He was rising to his feet even as Davidson and his sister entered the lounge. He moved toward them with uncertain footsteps.

'We must have a sitting-room,' he said. 'I cannot face these people. I'm beginning to feel a coward.'

Davidson went to the office, and very soon they found themselves upon the third floor, in an apartment overlooking Northumberland Avenue, gorgeous with plush and gilt mirrors, stiffly arranged chairs, an ornate chiffonnier. Haynes, who had come up in the lift muttering to himself, but obviously anxious for silence from his two companions, threw himself, almost as the door closed, upon the hard couch.

'I'm broken!' he cried out. 'I'm broken!'

Eileen sank on her knees by his side, her arms went round his neck. Davidson turned away and walked to the window a little awkwardly. Somehow he felt that it would be taking a mean advantage if he should look into her face, though all the time he was longing to see if her eyes had really softened, if those lips were really trembling a little, lips that were pressed to her brother's forehead.

'Brian,' she whispered, 'you mustn't! Bear up, please. Mr. Davidson is here. He's come with me. Sit up and talk to him.'

Haynes pulled himself together. He sat up, and Davidson, obeying a gesture from her, crossed the room once more.

'Brian,' he said, 'I'm very sorry to see you like this.'

'It's my first day out,' Haynes said. 'It's a little trying, you know, especially when the end is so near. I wanted just a few words with you, Malcolm. Good of you to come.'

Davidson nodded. 'I only wish there was something I could do,' he said.

'There is nothing,' said Haynes.

The girl turned away. 'When you want me, Brian,' she said softly, 'I'll be in the next room.'

'You might have some brandy brought up,' he said. 'I must talk for a few minutes, and I'm not feeling very strong.'

'I will ring the bell in the other room,' she said, 'and order it.'

She disappeared through the connecting door. Davidson, who had found himself watching her slow, even progress, turned once more to the man who sat by his side.

'I never thought I'd see you again,' Haynes started. 'I did my best, Davidson. I made friends with Austin all right - he was glad enough to have anyone to drink with - and before long he began to tell me about his claim to the Letlakana Mine.'

'Did he believe in it?' Davidson said.

'Absolutely,' Haynes said. 'I'm quite sure of that. He absolutely believed that directly he put it into the hands of any solicitor, you would have to come to him and buy, even though it cost you half your fortune. He was waiting those few days to see if you came.'

Davidson nodded. 'Tell me how it happened,' he said.

'It was like this,' Haynes continued, speaking hoarsely, and with difficulty, 'that night he wasn't quite so drunk. I pressed him a little too closely about his claim, and where he kept the paper. He was suddenly suspicious and quarrelsome. He tried to turn me out, and when I wanted to soothe him down, he struck me. He was a strong man and I was weak. I think that he meant to murder me. I remember I was half on the floor. My forehead was bleeding already, and he was coming towards me, shrieking with rage. 'I'm going to finish you!' he called out. Then I struck, hoping only to stun him, and, as you know, the blow killed him. I forgot for a moment about the paper. I thought only about making my escape. I had bad luck, and I did not succeed. I'm afraid it was a bungling sort of job, Davidson.'

'I'm very sorry indeed,' Davidson said, 'that I ever suggested it to you.'

'It wasn't your fault,' Haynes said. 'Nothing of this sort would have happened if he hadn't come for me. I meant to rob him if I could - I'll admit that - but no more. You see it was useless for me to try and open negotiations. He was too confident altogether. He spoke of a million pounds as his price. Tell me,' he went on, 'how do things stand now? Who has possession of the paper?'

Davidson hesitated for a moment. 'I do not know.'

Haynes's face fell. He seemed disappointed. 'I had an idea,' he said slowly, 'that you might have made some attempt to recover it. Everything was left in the room at the hotel for some time. It was easily done.'

'I did make an attempt,' Davidson said slowly. 'I have searched the room for that paper, but failed to find it.'

'You yourself?' Haynes said eagerly.

'Yes! I heard that there was a claimant coming for Austin's effects, and that they were going to be removed to Scotland Yard. I took a room at the hotel, and I got hold of a key. I went through everything the man had.'

'It was in the breast pocket of his grey coat, underneath the lining,' Haynes gasped.

'I found the place,' Davidson said, 'but it was empty.'

Haynes wiped the sweat from his forehead. His breathing was becoming difficult. Already the excitement was affecting him. 'But it was there on that night!' he said 'He took off his coat a few minutes before, and I saw him feel it in the lining.'

'All I can tell you,' Davidson said, 'is that the lining of the grey coat was torn, as though something had been abstracted. The paper was not there. It was not anywhere in the room. I ran a risk,' he continued, after a moment's pause, 'which I dare not think of, even now, but it was in vain. Someone had been before me.'

'Was there anyone else upon the scent, then?' Haynes said.

'Can you think of anyone?' Davidson said.

Haynes looked at him with distended eyes. 'You don't mean to insinuate,' he began, 'that I - that I had given it away?'

'Not wilfully,' Davidson said. 'Is there anyone at all to whom you spoke of this?'

Haynes shook his head. 'Only to my sister,' he said, 'and she is as silent as the grave.'

'Nevertheless,' Davidson said, 'the paper has gone. Someone has it - is holding it now - for a purpose, I suppose. There can but be one purpose. Perhaps,' he added, 'you had better ask your sister, to be quite sure whether she ever mentioned its existence to anyone.'

'We will ask her at once!' Haynes said 'I will ask her before you. Let me get up. Help me. I will fetch her.'

Davidson stretched out his hand. 'No!' he said. 'You must not excite yourself Haynes. I will knock at the door and call your sister.'

Haynes lay back, gasping. Davidson crossed the room and knocked at the door which led to the inner apartment.

'Miss Haynes,' he said.

She opened the door almost immediately. 'Yes?'

Davidson stood aside. 'Your brother,' he said, 'has a question to ask you!'

Chapter 25

Eileen came slowly into the room. It seemed to Davidson, watching her curiously, that she had been steeling herself to defiance. There was no change in her expression, and her lips seemed tighter drawn than ever. She went at once to her brother's side.

'You have been talking too much, Brian,' she said. 'You know that it is not good for you.'

He leaned across to the little table which stood by his side and helped himself to brandy. He was indeed looking terribly ill. The lines under his eyes seemed traced with a coal-black pencil, and his hand shook so that half the brandy was spilled.

'Eileen,' he said, 'I must ask you a question. You remember that I spoke to you of a document - Austin had it. I was trying to deal with him, trying to get it back for Mr. Davidson here.'

'Yes,' she said calmly, 'I remember your speaking of it.'

'We have reason to believe,' he continued, gasping a little, - 'reason to believe that it has been stolen. Mr. Davidson wants to know whether at any time you have mentioned its existence to anyone.'

She looked at Davidson and back at her brother. Her face was unchanged. 'No!' she said. 'I have mentioned it to no one.'

'You see,' her brother continued, 'it's like this. No one but I knew of that paper. Davidson here told me, and I told no one except you. And yet we have evidence, we know that it has been stolen from Austin's room since his death. That is why we want you to be quite sure that you did not mention its existence to anyone.'

'No mention of it has crossed my lips,' she said. 'I have no friends, no confidants. I have spoken to no one about it. Nothing in the world,' she continued, 'would be more improbable than that I'd have done so.'

He turned to Davidson, who stood by with impassive face. 'You hear?' he said 'You hear? I was quite sure about Eileen. She doesn't go talking about. She's no gossip, are you, Eileen?'

'I hope not,' she said.

'I have no reason, I'm sure,' Davidson said slowly, 'to doubt Miss Haynes's discretion.'

She raised her eyes for a moment, and met his. The faint satire in his tone was intentionally provocative, but it failed to move her. Her regard of him was entirely impersonal. He looked away with a light shrug of the shoulders.

'Well, Haynes,' he said, 'it seems there is nothing further to be done. If the paper does turn up,' he added, 'I'll know how to deal with its holder. In the meantime, about yourself.'

Haynes laughed a little hysterically. 'About myself,' he repeated. 'That's a fruitful subject, isn't it?'

'Doctors make mistakes sometimes,' Davidson said. 'Let us hope that they may have made one in your case. Anyhow, there is no reason why you should not be comfortable, and have the best medical advice. Go wherever you think best, and send me your address. I'll not forget that your accident took place when you were engaged upon my affairs.'

'You are very good, Davidson,' Haynes said.

The girl looked up. 'Mr. Davidson's kindness is quite unnecessary,' she said. 'We are in no want of money.'

'Your sister does not quite understand,' Davidson said, turning to him. 'We have been through too many rough times in Africa together to stand upon ceremony now. You will perhaps be able to explain to her later on.'

He took up his hat and turned toward the door. 'I'll expect to hear from you,' he said, 'as soon as you have decided where to go, - either from you, Haynes,' he added, shaking hands with him, 'or from your sister.'

'You are very kind, Davidson,' Haynes said. 'I'm sorry I have made such a mess of things.'

'It was not your fault,' Davidson said. 'Good-day, Miss Haynes!'

She looked at him for a moment, but she did not offer to take his outstretched hand. He smiled, and withdrew it at once.

'Good-day, Mr. Davidson!' she said.

The door closed behind him. Haynes was watching his sister anxiously. 'Eileen,' he said, 'what is the matter with you? You were scarcely civil to Mr. Davidson.'

'Oh! I think I was,' she said. 'In any case, we don't want to take alms from him, do we?'

'It isn't exactly that,' Haynes objected.

'It is.'

'He can afford it,' Haynes said. 'He is very rich. A thousand pounds to him is like sixpence to us.'

'It doesn't alter facts,' she replied. 'I do not like Mr. Davidson, Brian. It is through him that this trouble has come upon us. You've taken enough of his money.'

'And when I'm gone?' he said. 'What about you then?'

'Have I ever failed to make my own way?' she said quietly. 'I'll be safe enough, Brian.'

He started to cough, and very soon further speech was impossible. He was painfully exhausted. She sat by his side until he went off to sleep. Of his hopeless state there could no longer be any doubt. He was wasted almost to a shadow. Even in sleep his breath came heavily, and a fever seemed upon him. She stole softly from his side, and stood for a few minutes at the window, looking out. Below, the pulse of the great world was beating with the same maddening regularity. The stream of wayfarers swept on, the roar of traffic was as inevitable as the waves of the sea. She stood by the window with small, clenched hands. Behind her, his loud breathing seemed to beat out the time toward Death.

Davidson himself was one of those wayfarers, but at least his thoughts, as he was being whirled eastward in his taxi, were fixed upon the tragedy which he had left behind him. He knew very well that it was not a question of months but of days with Brian Haynes. Was it only for that that the girl was waiting? Her whole attitude towards him had about it a certain flavour of mystery which oppressed him. It was like trying to face an enemy hidden in a darkened room, listening for his footstep, not knowing whence the blow might fall. Notwithstanding the warm sunshine, he shivered a little as he descended from the taxi and entered his offices.

Chapter 26

The girl was sitting in the middle of a hard horsehair sofa, her elbows upon her knees, her head resting in her hands. She looked across the dreary apartment and out of the ill-cleaned windows, with dull, despairing eyes. This, then, was to be the end of her dreams. She must go back to the life which she felt to be intolerable, or she must throw herself headlong into the maelstrom.

There was one other occupant of the room, and, curiously enough, his attitude appeared to be a somewhat similar one. He was a short, thick-set young man, with brown moustache, flashily dressed, with a red tie, an imitation diamond, and soiled linen to further disfigure an appearance at no time particularly prepossessing. He was standing with his legs a little apart, looking out into the uninspiring street. His hands were thrust deep down into the pockets of his trousers. He had all the appearance of a man who finds the burden of life an unwelcome thing. Presently he began to whistle, not cheerfully, but some doleful air of sentimental import. The girl upon the couch seemed irritated. She herself was in the last stage of dejection, and the sound grew maddening.

'Oh, don't do that, please!' she exclaimed at last.

He turned around in amazement, for the first time realizing that he was not alone. 'I beg your pardon,' he said.

The girl remembered that he was a stranger to her, but after all, what did it matter?

'I asked you to stop whistling,' she said.

He said 'Certainly!' and continued to look at her.

'Sort of habit I get into,' he explained, 'when I'm down in the dumps.'

'Does it do you any good?' she said. 'If so, I'll learn how to whistle myself.'

'Meaning,' he said, 'that we are companions in - dumpiness?'

She shrugged her shoulders, but did not trouble to reply.

'I wish to God,' he exclaimed, 'I'd never left Cape Town!'

Then for the first time she looked at him with a gleam of interest, and said, 'Do you come from South Africa?'

He nodded. 'I did, and I only wish I were back there. I could always keep my head above water there, but London is a rotten hole. I suppose it's because I don't know the runs,' he added meditatively. 'Anyhow, it's broke me.'

She continued the conversation without feeling the slightest interest in it, but simply because it was an escape - a temporary escape - from her thoughts. 'What did you come over for?' she said.

'A fool's errand!' he said. 'I lent a man some money - a sort of speculation it was - and I came over to see how he was getting on.'

'And I suppose he'd lost it,' she said.

'He's lost himself,' said the man, 'which is about as bad. I wish I could lay my hands upon him. I'd get a bit of my own back, one way or another.'

'London is a big place,' she said. 'People are not easy to find unless you know all about them.'

'This man left South Africa only a month or so ago. He gave me an address here where he said I'd always hear of him. I've been there nearly every day. He turned up there all right regularly after he first landed. He hasn't been there at all for two months, and they haven't the least idea where he is.'

'You don't even know,' she said, 'whether the speculation is successful or not?'

He shook his head gloomily. 'It don't make much odds, so far as I can see,' he said. 'If it came off, he's bolted with the profits. If it didn't, he's hiding for fear I'll want my money back again. It's a rotten sort of show, anyway.'

'What was his name?' she said idly.

'His real name,' the man said, 'was the same as your own, - that is,' he added, 'I think I heard old Mrs. Tinsley call you Miss Austin, didn't I?'

She looked at him steadily for several moments without speaking. He couldn't fail to see the change in her face. Her lips were parted, her eyes were suddenly lit with an almost passionate fire. The change in her features was illuminating. She was no longer a tired, depressed-looking young woman of ill-tempered appearance. Her good looks had reasserted themselves.

'His real name was Austin,' she repeated softly. 'He came from South Africa. Tell me some more about him?'

167

'Why?' he said bluntly.

'Because,' she told him, 'my name is Hannah Austin, and I'm here on very much the same errand as you, only with this difference. I know where my uncle is. I know what has become of him.'

He came over from the window, and stood on the hearthrug by her side. Some part of her excitement had become communicated to him. 'I say,' he exclaimed, 'this is a rum go, and no mistake! If it's the same man, we may be able to help one another. It's Richard Austin I'm looking for, called over there Bully Austin. He was a man about fifty years old, been in South Africa for the last twenty years, a mine prospector and general adventurer. He'd had his fingers in a good many pies, had Richard.'

'What was he over in England for?' she said.

The young man hesitated. 'I don't know that there's any harm in telling you,' he said, 'only remember its information for information. I'm giving you the whole show away.'

'I'll tell you all you want to know,' she interrupted. 'Go on.'

'Well,' the young man said, 'he came over to lay claim to a Mine that he considered he'd been done out of.'

'A Mine!' the girl repeated breathlessly. 'Was it a rich one - very rich, I mean?'

'I'd say so,' the young man said. 'It was a complicated bit of business - the Mine's in other hands, you see - but Austin reckoned that he'd got a claim to it, anyway, and he expected either to be squared for a big amount, or to get a syndicate to take the thing up. He came to me dead on his uppers. My name's van Heerden. He and I had been pretty thick at odd times, and though we'd been in a good many deals together, we'd kept friends in a way. He came to me, as I say, in Cape Town, and he told me what the game was. He wanted a matter of two or three hundred pounds to get over to this side, and to start things properly. Well, I thought it out, and though it was about all I was worth in the world, I let him have it. Over he comes. I got a letter from him to say he'd landed, and never another line. I cabled - no answer. Over I came myself, for he'd scarcely left Cape Town before a little affair that I was mixed up in went plumb wrong, and I lost every penny I'd got left. So over here I come, and I've been here a fortnight, and I tell you Austin seems to have vanished from the face of the earth. The worst of it is,' he continued, 'I'm skint. I've got to leave this place today because I can't pay my bill, and I've no idea where to raise a sovereign.'

The girl's sense of humour triumphed for a second over her excitement. 'There are your diamonds,' she reminded him. 'I heard you talking about them at dinner the other night. One of them you said was worth a hundred pounds.'

'A bluff,' he said readily. 'They are false, every one of them. I talked like that to get old mother Tinsley to let my account go on a bit, but she wasn't having any. Now, I say, I've told you my story. Tell me why you are so keen on knowing about it.'

'Yes,' she said, 'I will tell you. My name is Hannah Austin, and I'm the niece of the man whom you have come to England to find.'

He made use of an oath for which he forgot even to apologize. 'You know where he is!' he said 'Come, remember it was a fair bargain. Information for information!'

'He is dead!'

The young man staggered back. His first emotion of shocked surprise lasted only a few seconds. Anger and disappointment took its place. 'Dead?' he said 'And my money - what about that? What he left belongs to me, anyway. It's got to be made up. I can show you his note for it.'

'You had better wait,' she said coldly, 'Until I have told you everything. I suppose you don't read the papers?'

'Never,' he said. 'What good are they to me?'

'They might have been of some use on the present occasion,' she said. 'They might at any rate have saved you from wasting a good deal of time. My uncle was murdered in the Hotel Universal by a man named Haynes.'

The young man swore again, - fluently, volubly, - swore until he had come to the end of a varied and extensive vocabulary. When he had finished, there was an excited flush in his cheeks and a bright light in his eyes. 'By Haynes - Brian Haynes?' he said 'He was one of us out there when we were prospecting up the Newsom Valley. Look here,' he continued, 'you and I have got to have this out. Murdered, was he? Well, I'm the man that may be able to throw some light upon that. What's happened to Haynes? Had he anything to say?'

'I will tell you all that I know,' the girl said. 'My uncle wrote me directly he arrived in England. He told me that he had been fortunate in Africa, that he had come to take possession

170

of a large fortune, and that he would be sending for me in a very short time to live with him, and that, as he had no other relative, I'd be rich all my days. I replied, of course, asking whether I could not come at once. He wrote me again to tell me to wait for a day or two, until his affairs were settled. Then I heard no more. I waited. I wrote again. I waited, and wrote again. There was no reply. I found afterwards that my letters had never even been called for at the address where he told me to write. Then one day a stranger told my uncle there to look at the papers. We found the story of his murder. He had been dead some time.'

'Haynes was tried, I suppose?' the man said. 'Did he say what his motive was? Has he been hanged?'

'He insisted upon it that it was a quarrel,' the girl said. 'I do not believe him. He was found guilty and reprieved. I saw in the papers last night that he had been released. I believe that he has only a few days to live.'

'And you?' the young man said.

'I came up,' the girl said slowly, 'to take possession of my uncle's effects.'

'Have you got them?' he said breathlessly.

'Yes!' the girl said.

'There were papers?' he said.

'Some,' she said, 'but none of any importance.'

He looked at her suspiciously. She shrugged her shoulders. 'Look here,' she said, 'I'm telling you the truth. Look at me, look at my gloves - mended half-a-dozen times. Look at my clothes, just hanging on my back and no more. If there had been a single thing amongst my uncle's papers on which I could have raised even a five-pound note, do you think that I'd be sitting here like this, wondering which might be the quickest way out of the world?'

The young man moistened his lips. He was obviously in a state of excitement. 'Listen,' he said, 'among these papers was there a sort of deed on yellow parchment paper, roughly written, with a government stamp in the left-hand corner, a paper which spoke of a Mine called the Letlakana Mine?'

She shook her head decidedly. 'There was nothing of the sort.'

Then the young man swore again, and this time he seemed to surpass himself. 'Your uncle was robbed!' he exclaimed, - 'robbed of that paper! I tell you,' he added, 'he was murdered for it, and for no other reason!'

'How do you know?' the girl cried.

'Why, it's as simple as A B C,' he explained. 'He had the paper in his possession when he came to England. The mine has been claimed by a great syndicate who are working it now. He came to see them, to make terms. The next thing we hear is that he is murdered and the paper is gone. They thought that no one else knew of it. Young lady,' he exclaimed, 'you may thank your stars, as I do, that you and me have come together. We'll have justice, and we'll have that fortune yet!'

Chapter 27

With his feet to the sea, and his head pillowed by many cushions, Haynes lay in a long invalid chair at the edge of the little strip of shingle which separated the tower from the sea. Every limb was at rest, every nerve seemed lulled into quiescence. The sun and wind had left their traces upon his hollow cheeks. It seemed, indeed, as though Death had lifted her hand from his forehead. It was only when one looked closer that one realized his terrible weakness, realized how slender, indeed, the thread was by which he held on to life. There was scarcely a breath of wind stirring. The sun was high in the heavens, and the whole country seemed lulled into a state of almost unnatural repose. The distant trees were motionless, as though, indeed, they were simply painted things against that background of deep blue sky. The smoke from the little cluster of cottages crept upwards, straight as a ruled line. The cattle in the fields seemed all asleep, exhausted by the unexpected heat. The sea was like a lake, almost placid.

The man dozed, and Eileen sat by his side, with her eyes fixed steadily and yet absently upon the distant horizon. A week, at most, the doctor had given him, and after that - what? She looked backwards to the window, - the window through which she had entered on that wild night earlier in the year. She looked away again uneasily. She was afraid of such moments as these. It was to escape from them that she had protested so vehemently against their accepting Davidson's offer of his cottage.

At low tide, a rough, pebbly road led from the village to the cottage, as well as the dyke footpath higher up. Along this came two people, a man and a woman, mere specks at first in the distance, but rapidly becoming more and more evident. They walked fast, and they looked always anxiously toward the tower, which stood out at the end of the road against the background of the sky, - a curious, almost uncanny, sort of building.

'If they see us coming,' said Hannah Austin, 'they will certainly try to prevent our seeing him. Our only chance is to come upon them unexpectedly. They can watch the dyke path from the front, but few people ever come by this road. It winds about so, and it is generally thick with sea mud.'

The man nodded. He too was keeping his gaze fixed in a strained manner upon their goal. 'Now that we are so near,' he said, 'so near to him, we will make him speak. We will not be driven away. He cannot escape from us there.'

There was a curious air of determination about these two, a certain grimness which seemed common to both of them, as they hurried along the rough, stone-strewn road. They had reached the last hundred yards now, and their course was perfectly straight. They walked single file along the little stretch of marshland which served as a footpath.

'He's in front, lying on a chair,' she whispered. 'They won't be able to get him in now before we are there.'

The road terminated suddenly upon the beach. The man and the girl scrambled up a little shingle mound. When at last Eileen heard the sounds of their approach, they were already between her and the house. Any attempt at escape was useless. She came a few steps toward them.

'Who are you, please, and what do you want?' she said quickly.

Van Heerden stretched out a hand toward the prone figure of Haynes, who was lying there still with closed eyes. 'We want a few words with your brother,' he said. 'We shall not keep him long, but it is very important. We have come a long way to see him.'

'It is impossible,' she said firmly. 'He is very ill indeed. The doctor allows him to see no one. I don't know how you found your way here, but you must please return at once.'

'I have come a long way,' van Heerden said slowly.

'I'm sorry,' she said, 'but can't you see that it makes no difference? If you were to ask him questions, he is not well enough to answer you - scarcely to understand. Any sudden shock at all - even a recognition - might kill him.'

Van Heerden hesitated no longer. He pushed Eileen away, and motioned to Hannah to follow him. At that moment Haynes opened his eyes and turned his head. Van Heerden walked towards him and leaned over his chair.

'You remember me, Haynes?' he said. 'My name is van Heerden, Steve van Heerden. We were up the Kloof Valley together, camped out, you know, at Prince's Gorge, for more than a month, - you and I and Davidson, and a lot of us.'

'I remember,' Haynes faltered, trying to raise himself. 'Yes, I remember!'

He had a fit of coughing. Eileen passed her arms around him and held him up. 'If you stay,' she whispered to van Heerden, 'you will kill him. He ought not to speak ever a sentence.'

'It isn't much we want him to say, miss,' van Heerden said doggedly, 'but there's a question he's got to answer. If he is as near death as you say, it can't make much difference what happens, and it means more than death to me and to this young lady.'

Haynes had recovered sufficiently to drink from a glass which Eileen had handed to him. He turned once more toward van Heerden. 'That is all finished,' he said painfully, - 'those days. I'm ill, - too ill to talk, too ill to think, too ill to live! Please go.'

Van Heerden bent over him. 'Haynes,' he said, 'you and I were never enemies, even if we didn't exactly hit it off together. Listen to me for a moment. Austin borrowed my last three hundred pounds in Cape Town to come over here and lay claim to the Letlakana Mine. He had the government deed with him. I have seen it. I followed him over to claim my share, and I found him dead, killed, and the paper gone. I'm not asking you to give away your game, whatever it was, but we want the paper. This is Austin's niece with me, and I'm his partner. We inherit his claim to the Letlakana Mine, and we want that document.'

'The document was not amongst Austin's effects when they were examined after his death,' Haynes said. 'I did not take it. I do not know what has become of it. That is the truth. Leave me alone now. I cannot talk any more.'

His head dropped back upon his pillow. He was white to the lips. Eileen hurried to his side. Once more she turned upon the two.

'Are you satisfied?' she cried. 'You have nearly killed him - for nothing. I know very well that no document of any sort such as you describe has been found. If Mr. Austin ever had it, it was probably stolen from him.'

'Stolen, yes!' van Heerden said, - 'stolen right enough! That is what we are here about. This young lady is his niece, and I'm his partner. What was left behind belongs to us, and, so far as I know, the only thing worth having was that document. We want it, and, by God,' he wound up, 'we've got to have it!'

'Do you imagine,' the girl said, without change of countenance, 'that you will find it here?'

'I will tell you what I do imagine,' van Heerden said. 'Men don't commit murder for nothing. Your brother tried to steal that paper, or rather he did steal it. The game's up now. He's no opportunity to make use of it, and it belongs to us. It belongs to us and we've come for it. There, now you know the truth. We've come for it, and we won't stop until we get it.'

Haynes raised himself a little in his seat. 'Van Heerden,' he said, 'it's no use talking like that. I haven't got it. I'll be frank, frank as you have been. I know no more than you do who has got it. I quarrelled with Austin, and he got suspicious. We fought in his room, and the result you know, but I was arrested before I left the hotel. Everyone knows that. The paper - I never had it - I never even saw it. Where it is now God only knows. I don't.'

Haynes fell back in his chair, coughing violently. For several moments he was incapable of speech. Eileen knelt by his side. When he had finished coughing, she held a wineglass to his lips and made him sip its contents. He lay back now as though completely exhausted. She turned to face these unwelcome visitors.

'You see,' she cried, pointing to him, 'a little more of this and you will kill him. Go away, both of you. He has nothing to tell you.'

Van Heerden laughed a little brutally. 'Come,' he said, 'this game won't do. We are here for the truth, not to be put off with these fairy-tales. It is the truth we want, and the truth we'll have, or I'll wring it out of him even if it kills him.'

Haynes's eyes were closed, and he showed no sign of having heard. Eileen stood up boldly before him. 'You are fools!' she said. 'He has told you all he knows. If Austin ever had the deed you speak of, he parted with it to someone else, not to my brother.'

'Someone else!' van Heerden repeated. 'Do you take us for fools? If he parted with that deed, he parted with it for a fortune. Where's the money? Show us the deed or the money, and we are satisfied. Show us neither, and we'll not leave this place until he has spoken.'

A step upon the shingle behind suddenly diverted their attention. The eyes of every one of them were fixed upon the tall figure who was walking swiftly up the slope. They had been so engrossed that they had not even heard the sound of the motor-car which was standing there, splashed with mud, and with its engine still panting. With his glasses in his hand, and his long grey coat thrown open, Malcolm Davidson strode up to them.

'Come,' he said, 'it seems to me that I have arrived opportunely. What does this mean? Who are these people? Miss Austin, is this man your companion? What does he mean by speaking in such a tone to a dying man?'

Van Heerden stood as though turned to stone, but his eyes never left Davidson's.

Chapter 28

Hannah Austin leaned forward and touched her companion's back as they drove through the village. 'Look,' she said. 'You see that cottage we are just passing? That is where I have lived for the last four years.'

Van Heerden followed her outstretched finger. He saw the little grove of bare trees, and the marshland stretching out beyond to the bare sea. 'Winter and summer?' he said.

'Winter and summer.'

He nodded. 'About time you went fortune-hunting!' he said.

No other word passed between them until they reached the railway station. They descended from the car, and watched it almost immediately swing round and disappear.

'So this is the end of our little excursion,' Hannah said.

'Yes!' van Heerden said. 'Aren't you satisfied?'

'Why should I be?' she said. 'What have we gained?'

Van Heerden drew a long breath. 'Ah, I forgot!' he said. 'You don't understand.'

He drew her into the refreshment room. She declined to drink, but she sat in a corner while he disposed of several whiskies and sodas. At first he would say nothing, and she waited. Presently he began.

'You think,' he said, 'that I was a coward, because when Davidson bundled us off in his car and told the man to drive us to the nearest railway station, I did not protest. You think that I'd have made a scene there? It wasn't worthwhile. Davidson's coming gave the whole game away. Don't you understand?'

'Not a word,' she said.

'Listen, then. Malcolm Davidson is the man who is supposed to be the owner of the Letlakana Mine, which was really your Uncle Austin's.'

She looked at him with gleaming eyes. 'Say that again,' she said. 'I don't quite understand.'

'The deed which is missing from your Uncle Austin's effects,' van Heerden said slowly, 'is the title-deed to the Letlakana Mine. That mine was illegally taken possession of by Malcolm Davidson. He sold it to the company, of which he is now president, at an enormous price. He is the man with whom your Uncle Austin came to England to treat. Austin was murdered. By whom? By Haynes. Who was at the back of Haynes? Whose tool was he? We know! Chance this afternoon made everything clear to us. Can't you see that Haynes killed your uncle and stole that deed to save Malcolm Davidson from ruin, - at his bidding, as his accomplice?'

'It takes my breath away,' the girl said. 'Now I think of it, of course, it is Davidson's cottage they are in. He was there himself only a few weeks ago. It was through him that we heard of my uncle's murder.'

'The whole thing's as simple as A B C,' van Heerden said. 'Can't you see that Davidson has given himself into our hands? Of course Haynes stole the deed! Of course Davidson has it! He will have to pay for our silence! By God, he will have to pay!'

The girl looked up from her seat on the leather couch, looked at her companion long and critically. 'Do you think we can hold our own against a man like Malcolm Davidson?'

'It depends upon the cards, and they are in our hands. We must go back to London. We must wait till he is at his office. Then I will see him. You can leave the thing in my hands now. I'll know how to approach him. He cannot deny his friendship with the Haynes. They are occupying, even at this moment, his own cottage. Very likely I'll be able to discover other things connecting him with them. The newspapers you showed me spoke of great influence which was brought to bear on the granting of the reprieve. We may find that Malcolm Davidson was at the back of that. Anyhow, he is connected closely enough with them. I'm here, ready to swear that when Austin left Africa he left with the original title-deed of the Letlakana Mine in his pocket. I think that the friendship between his murderer and Malcolm Davidson, who sold that mine for close upon a million pounds, is a thing that will need a little explanation.'

'And in the meantime,' said the girl bitterly, 'we are starving.'

'Not quite,' he said. 'We have one hundred pounds. That will take us back to London, and find us rooms somewhere for the night. We must scrape along somehow until I can get to Davidson's offices.'

'You are not forgetting,' the girl said, 'that the thirty-eight shillings you are speaking of is my property?'

'We are partners,' van Heerden said. 'You shall carry the purse if you will, but there is no object in it.'

'You seem to do most of the spending,' she reminded him. 'If you think that we can afford it,' she added, glancing at his empty glasses, 'I'd like a cup of tea.'

He ordered it at once, and sat down by her side. 'Look here,' he said, 'I don't see what you want to be so blooming stand-off for. Times are a bit rough with us just now, but, you mark my word, we shall pull through all right. This man Davidson is in the hollow of our hands. He has been Haynes's accomplice. No one who knows the facts could possibly doubt it. A word from us would ruin him.'

The girl sighed. She had drawn a little away from the man. 'Do you believe, then,' she said, 'that Mr. Davidson has the deed?'

'Either that, or it is destroyed,' said van Heerden. 'But don't bother about that. Whether the deed is still existing or not, we know enough to make it worth his while to buy us, even though it costs him half his fortune.'

'In the meantime,' the girl said, 'please get the tickets. The train will be in, in a few minutes.'

'Come with me,' he said suspiciously. 'Remember, we're partners.'

'Oh! We are partners right enough,' she said, rising and following him out of the place. 'You needn't be afraid that I'm going to let you go. Just now you are all that stands between me and a return.'

On the way up to town he began to build castles. He was optimistic, sanguine in the extreme. The girl listened almost stolidly. Her companion had begun to depress her. He was badly dressed, his linen was soiled, his imitation jewellery was hideous. He sat opposite her in the train, and there were things in his face from which she shrank. She was more than thankful that they were not alone.

'Are you tired, or what?' he said at last, a little sullenly. 'Surely I made it all plain enough? You don't doubt that there's money in this for us?'

'There should be,' she admitted slowly. 'And yet -'

'And yet what?'

'I have seen Mr. Davidson before,' she said hesitatingly. 'I have talked with him once or twice. Somehow or other, when I think that it may come to be a struggle between you and him -'

He interrupted her with a brazen laugh. 'You think I won't be able to stand up against him! Well, you shall see. There's a good deal in holding the cards, you know.'

'You haven't the deed,' she reminded him.

'I don't want it,' he said. 'I'm not afraid of Malcolm Davidson. I have known him a good many years, and he knows me. We are up against one another now, and you may fancy his chances; but I tell you my back's against the wall, and his isn't. He's there fighting in the open. I've got him, I tell you, - got him!'

She half closed her eyes. This was not the way in which she had hoped to come into her fortune. In her heart, she could not believe a word he said. Davidson was a strong man; van Heerden, she was already beginning to discover, was nothing but a bully and a craven. If it came to a duel between the two, she found it easier to believe that van Heerden would be worsted.

At King's Cross Station they separated. Van Heerden, a little sulkily, accepted his dismissal, and parted with half of the money which he had.

'You can go where you choose,' she said. 'You can come back to Mrs. Towsley's, if you like, but I tell you frankly that except while we are on business I think it better that we should stay apart.'

'I can't see why,' he muttered.

'For one thing,' she said, 'we might be taken for adventurers. I do not know much about the law, but it seems to me you won't be very far out of its clutches when your negotiations with Mr. Davidson begin.'

'I can take care of myself,' he said gruffly. 'Can I see you back to the old lady's, anyhow?'

'No!' she said. 'I would rather go alone.'

'Come and have one drink in the refreshment room, just to wish ourselves luck,' he begged.

She went in with him and drank a cup of coffee. He had two liqueurs, and would have had more, but she dragged him sharply away.

'Remember,' she said, 'that I have nothing more I can raise money on. These few shillings are all we have. If Mr. Davidson does not return for several days, we must leave.'

'Davidson will come back,' he said, with a defiant laugh. 'I let him have things his own way today, but he knows just where he is. Mark my words, he will be at the office tomorrow morning, and he will be there expecting to see me.'

Chapter 29

Van Heerden was too hopeful. It was three days before he was able to see Malcolm Davidson. During that three days he had lived on a few shillings, spent mostly in drinks. He swaggered into Davidson's office, an untidy, dissolute-looking creature. His efforts to seem at his ease were almost ludicrous.

'A bit different, this, to the Newsom Valley,' he said, as he sat down without waiting for an invitation. 'Things have gone pretty well with you, eh, Davidson? Slap-up offices you've got, and the chink of money everywhere. It reminds me of what I've come about.'

'You have come for money, have you?' Davidson said.

'Well, I don't know about that. I don't know how you look at it, but it seems to me that there's a bit owing, a bit which might come my way. I'd tell you, perhaps, that I'm representing Miss Austin as well as myself.'

'Richard Austin's niece?' Davidson said.

'Exactly. She is heiress to anything the old man had, and I was partner with him in the Letlakana Mine.'

'In what?' Davidson said.

'In the Letlakana Mine,' van Heerden repeated distinctly.

Davidson leaned back in his chair. 'I must ask you to explain yourself,' he said. 'The Letlakana Mine belongs to the syndicate of which I'm a director.'

'That's all very well for a bluff,' said van Heerden, 'but you got rid of Austin a little too easily.'

'Got rid of him?'

'Oh! I'm not thinking of this last time,' van Heerden interrupted, with a hard laugh. 'I'm thinking of the time he put you on to the mine, and you took possession of it.'

'It was perfectly legal,' Davidson said.

'Perhaps so, - perhaps it wasn't,' van Heerden said. 'Anyway, I know very well, and so, probably, do you, that Austin left South Africa six months ago, with the government title-deed of the Letlakana Mine in his pocket. I advanced him the money to come, and he made me his partner.'

'These are amazing statements of yours,' Davidson said. 'May I ask where this wonderful deed is?'

'You may ask,' van Heerden said, 'but not me. Better go to Haynes. He knows, though he keeps his lips tight shut. He knows, and so do you! Never mind about that. You don't want a lawsuit, - no more do we.'

'Who are 'we'?' Davidson said.

'Miss Austin and myself,' van Heerden said. 'We are partners in this. I have come to you as a reasonable man. Austin landed in this country with the title-deeds of the mine which you have always considered yours, in his pocket. Today he is murdered, and his papers have disappeared. He was murdered by Haynes, whom you are now befriending.

188

There's a story there for the newspapers, - there's something more than a story, Davidson.'

'Do I understand,' Davidson said calmly, -

'You can understand what you please,' van Heerden said. 'I want my money back, and I want big interest. And then there's the girl. She should be standing at this moment in your shoes. Half of the Letlakana Mine is hers by right. It is for you to say what it would be worth your while to put down to close this business.'

'Now,' Davidson said suavely, 'you are talking common sense. But what I'd like to know is, where is this wonderful title-deed?'

'Oh, damn you, it's in the fire, I suppose!' van Heerden cried. 'You and he know. Haynes's your man, and he's the sort to die game. But he didn't kill Austin for nothing. I wouldn't mind betting that that deed has been burnt to ashes, but even then, I know a little too much, eh?'

Davidson shrugged his shoulders. 'You know a great deal too much,' he said. 'I'm to understand, then, finally, that you want me to buy your silence?'

'Put it that way if you choose,' van Heerden said, 'only I warn you that I haven't come here on a child's game. This is a big business, - a big business for me and for the girl. She must have her share, and I mine.'

'And the amount?'

'One millionpounds. Remember that it has to be divided.'

'In other words,' said Davidson, 'I'm to buy your silence as to these matters upon which you have spoken, for the sum of one million pounds?'

'It is too little,' van Heerden said. 'The mine is worth ten times as much - the mine and your position.'

'If I give you this sum,' Davidson said, 'do I understand that it closes the whole affair? You must remember that I do not admit having even seen this deed you spoke of. Supposing it turns up in somebody else's hands?'

Van Heerden laughed ironically. 'We'll guarantee you against that,' he said.

'That's easy to say,' Davidson objected, 'but I don't see how. Come, I will be perfectly truthful. I haven't got that deed. If it should be still in existence, and be used against me after I have paid you this sum of money, I'd be in somewhat an unfortunate position.'

'There isn't the slightest fear of it,' van Heerden said. 'Besides -'

'Besides what?' Davidson said, looking up from his desk.

'It isn't as though the deed were a certainty,' he said slowly. 'Of course, the law is a little complicated. There would be witnesses on both sides, and the case might go anyhow.'

'It would depend a little, I think,' Davidson said quietly, 'on which side you gave evidence for. I think you could upset that deed if you chose.'

'Perhaps I could,' van Heerden said gruffly.

'Will you do it,' Davidson said, 'if it should ever be set into action against me? Remember that even though I know you will not believe me, the fact remains that although I have defended Haynes, I'm not in possession of that deed.'

Van Heerden leaned across from his chair. 'Listen, Davidson,' he said. 'I'm not here to bluff about that wonderful document. Perhaps it isn't worth the paper it's written on. Anyhow, here's my word for it. I'll see if ever an action is brought against you on the strength of that deed, that you blow it all sky high in five minutes.'

'Is the deed a forgery?' Davidson said.

Van Heerden did not answer.

'Or is it only the date?' Davidson continued.

Still van Heerden was silent. Then, 'There is no necessity,' he said, after a pause, 'of putting these things into plain words. You have only to find the money, and your anxieties are over.'

Davidson touched a bell by his side. 'Yours, I'm afraid,' he said, 'are only just beginning!'

The curtains behind were suddenly thrown aside. A tall, spare-looking man stepped out. Davidson turned towards him.

'Inspector,' he said, 'I give this man in charge for a barefaced attempt at blackmailing me. You have heard all that has been said. I don't think that there is anything for me to add.'

He rang the bell by his side a second time. A moment later a policeman entered from the outer office. Van Heerden, who had sprung to his feet, was glaring at them both, white with passion.

'So this is your game, Davidson!' he said 'By the Lord, you shall pay for it! You to dare to use the law against me, - you, who sent Haynes like a paid assassin to murder Austin!'

'A gross calumny,' Davidson said calmly. 'I had no interest in Austin's life or death.'

'It's a damned lie!' cried van Heerden. 'If you are going to do any arresting, inspector, arrest that man!' he cried, pointing with his fat white forefinger to where Davidson stood, debonair and well-dressed as usual, and with a little bunch of violets in his buttonhole. 'I tell you that he paid the man Haynes to kill Bully Austin in the Universal Hotel. I tell you I can prove it. I can prove this - that Austin left South Africa six months ago, with the deeds of the Letlakana Mine, which this man dared to sell as being his own at close upon a million pounds less than six months ago. I can tell you more! - '

They led him from the room, still shouting. At the door he turned back. 'It's a bold game this, Davidson,' he cried, 'but by heavens I'll cry quits with you before long! You think you have a case against me. I'm only certain of one thing, and that is that you have driven a nail into your own coffin. If I could only get at you, you - you blackguard!'

His eyes were bloodshot. He strained and struggled to free himself from the grasp of the two men.

'I'd kill you where you stand!' he cried. 'Do you think that I can be muzzled? Do you think that the truth won't come to light? People shall know it even if I never leave off telling it till my last breath comes.'

Davidson listened to him with immovable face. They got him outside at last. He heard him being dragged down the corridor, protesting all the time. Then he resumed his seat. 'It's a bold game to play,' he said to himself thoughtfully, 'and yet, if they really haven't the deed, there was nothing else to be done!'

Chapter 30

'I asked you to lunch at the club, Malcolm,' said Sir Andrew Linton, 'because I thought that we could talk here without being interrupted. If you came to Cavendish Square, Catherine would walk you right away from the table, and if I said to have a chat with you alone, there would be a perfect avalanche of questions to face.'

Davidson looked up a little curiously. For the first time he realized that this was not simply a casual invitation. His prospective father-in-law had really something to say to him.

'There was some matter which you wished to discuss, then?' Davidson said. 'I need scarcely say that I'm quite at your service.'

They were nearing the end of a very excellent luncheon. 'Well,' he said, 'there were a few things I wanted to say to you. You see, Davidson, the city is no longer a mythical place to us idlers. We meet people whose life is centred in money-making, every day. I have friends, friends beside yourself, who come from Lombard Street, and one hears things, gossip, I mean, and stray talk.'

Davidson seemed suddenly to recede into himself. His host noticed the change, and blamed himself for his want of tact. Nevertheless, as he had begun, so he went on.

'You see, Davidson,' he continued, 'Catherine is my only daughter, and it makes one more than ordinarily cautious. This blackmailing case of yours has set people talking a bit. Of course, I think you were right. It was a brave and sportsmanlike thing to do. The man is committed for trial, and I only hope he'll get penal servitude. All the same, there are a lot of people, you know, Davidson, who don't take quite the same view of it.'

'Naturally,' Davidson assented. 'One can scarcely occupy such a position as mine without having enemies. There are wheels within wheels in the financial world, you know, Sir Andrew Linton, just as there are in the social world. There are a dozen men who covet my post, and as many hundreds of hangers-on and parasites who would be glad to see me out of it.'

'Quite so,' said Sir Andrew Linton. 'Of course, this man van Heerden's attitude was distinctly belligerent, and his solicitors evidently knew what they were talking about when they reserved his defence. Tell me, when Austin came to you first had he really any papers at all which were likely to cause you embarrassment?'

'He had an original claim to the Letlakana Mine,' Davidson admitted, 'but it had lapsed before I took possession. It was not worth the paper it was written on.'

'Still, he had got that document?' Sir Andrew Linton said.

'Without a doubt,' Davidson said.

'You have no idea, I suppose, what became of it?' Sir Andrew Linton said.

'Not the slightest,' replied Davidson. 'I only know that it was not found among his effects.'

'Would it have been of any interest to you to secure it?' Sir Andrew Linton continued.

'I would have given a few hundred - perhaps a few thousand - pounds for it,' Davidson said, 'partly as a curiosity, partly in order to save any possible trouble.'

'Of course,' Sir Andrew Linton said, leaning back in his chair and sipping his coffee, 'the world is full of people who love to gossip, and you cannot gossip unless you invent ill about someone. Somehow or other, it never amuses people to talk good of their friends; conversation only becomes interesting when one can associate evil with them. There are things being said in connection with this van Heerden affair, Davidson, which are not altogether pleasant.'

'Go on,' Davidson said.

'For instance,' his host continued, 'I was told last night that van Heerden's tale was in substance true, - he did advance this man Austin money to come to England and assert his right to the Letlakana Mine. Austin was murdered with this deed in his possession, and it is freely whispered that you have befriended Haynes - his murderer. The paper has disappeared. We know that. Still, there is a further rumour that it may turn up at his trial. In that case, wouldn't you be rather badly hit?'

Davidson shrugged his shoulders. 'The exact facts are these,' he said. 'Austin's claim to the Letlakana Mine is worth very little. Nevertheless, he knew that any action he might take against me in the present state of our money market here would be somewhat disastrous. It would upset our credit and bring down our prices. Therefore, his idea, without a doubt, was to come to England and make a bargain with me. He didn't expect the mine. What he wanted was blood money. He came, and, perhaps unwisely, I would have nothing to do with him. Haynes was known to both of us out there. He came to see me a few days afterwards, and I commissioned him to buy this deed, if he could. He went to look for Austin, they drank together, an old quarrel was revived, and they fought. The end of that you know. Where the document has gone to, I can't imagine, but I can assure you that it was never meant to be the basis of a serious claim, merely the foundation stone of a perfect system of blackmailing. If I had listened for five minutes to van Heerden I'd have been in his power all my life. I'd have lost my self-respect. Very soon I'd have lost my nerve. I couldn't do it. I preferred to face him in a court of justice. He came to blackmail me, and he deserved to be punished. If he can prove that it is I who am the ill-doer, I will take my punishment. I can say no more.'

'You talk,' Sir Andrew Linton said, looking at him kindly, 'as I would have my own son talk. And yet, Davidson, this whole affair is distressing to me. I tell you frankly that it has upset all the pleasure with which I consented to your engagement. I cannot bear that anyone associated with Catherine should ever find himself in such a position. This case, of course, may go all in your favour, or it may not. If it does not, well, you know very well that it would be the beginning of very unpleasant things.'

'Does Catherine know of this little luncheon party of ours, Sir Andrew Linton?' Davidson said.

'She does not,' Sir Andrew Linton asserted. 'Catherine is, above all things, staunch. She is, I believe, too, sincerely attached to you. I'm speaking entirely for myself. I'm speaking, too, as the father of an only daughter, whose engagement to you was, after all, a little experimental. I'd like to see my daughter released from that engagement, Davidson.'

Davidson smoked steadily for several minutes. Finally, 'this is a little hard on me, isn't it, sir? I have only done what you yourself would have done - refused to have underhand dealings with men who made dishonourable propositions to me.'

'It is hard on you, Davidson,' Sir Andrew Linton said. 'It is very hard indeed. But remember, I never wanted Catherine to marry anyone in the city. I know you, and I like you. If you came to me with your hands clean and plenty of money, I'd not hesitate for a second, for I believe that Catherine likes you. But I hate scandal, I hate gossip, I hate notoriety! This blackmailing case of yours is going to result in all three. I'd like to go home and lay the case before Catherine, and have your permission to say that if it seems good to her mother and myself, the engagement between you two is broken.'

Davidson leaned back in his chair. It seemed to him that he had so little time to give to thoughts outside the immediate trend of the day's work. It was proposed that his engagement with Catherine should be broken. What did it mean to him, this engagement? How far into his life had she come? What place did she hold in his heart? His thoughts travelled backwards. He remembered his almost meteor-like accession to wealth and influence. He remembered how all doors had flown open to him. He remembered and realized exactly where he stood. He thought of Catherine. He remembered the first day when he had decided that she was the woman who would look well at the head of his table, who would be a pleasant companion for him, and would insure his having friends, when he gave up his struggling, amongst, the class of people with whom he desired to associate. It was in that way that he had looked at it from the first. Was it the same now? He had touched her hands. He had even kissed her lips. She had come into his arms and allowed him to embrace her, without any obvious reluctance. Only a few weeks ago she had kissed him voluntarily, absolutely of her own will. During their fortnight in Scotland she had shown herself more feminine than he had ever believed her. She had insisted upon taking him for walks by herself. She had taken his arm, encouraged him to make love to her, had deserted the bridge table in the evenings to sit in dark corners with him, had allowed him to hold her hand, even to snatch a few kisses. If she did not care for him, at least she was very near it. And as for him, - he was fond of her, without a doubt. Somewhere in the background of his apprehension there was some shadowy idea of a greater thing than this, a love more thrilling, more passionate, more mysterious, - music in the veins, which no Lady Catherine in the world had ever created. But there was about these thoughts something absolutely unreal, fantastic. They had never taken to themselves shape, never become associated with any human being. They were nothing to trust to, he told himself, - nothing. He looked out of the rain-swept window of the club. Curiously enough, he had a sudden vision of Eileen Haynes's quiet, set face. The memory of one passionate moment seemed suddenly to creep along his heartstrings like the wind over the strings of a harp. Such folly, he thought, frowning! Such absolute folly!

'Sir Andrew Linton,' he said at last, 'I'm only anxious to do what Lady Catherine wishes. If you will go home and tell her exactly what you have told me, I'd like you to add that it is only her happiness that I wish, and that if she desires to release me, I'll accept her decision without a murmur.'

Sir Andrew Linton played with his coffee-spoon nervously. 'I knew you'd say something like that, Davidson,' he said. 'Of course, it will not be easy. I believe that my daughter is really fond of you, and our influence over her, both her mother's and mine, is somewhat limited. You wouldn't feel inclined, I suppose, to come over to our side, to realize that under the circumstances an alliance between you and her could scarcely be a satisfactory thing, - in short, to encourage her to bring it to an end?'

'In other words,' Davidson said, 'you propose that instead of suffering myself to be jilted by Lady Catherine, I'd offer myself as a victim?'

'It's asking a good deal, I know,' Sir Andrew Linton said, 'and, of course, it all depends upon how you feel about it. But I tell you frankly, I can't help thinking - you must realize a little that this blackmailing case, even if it turns out well, is bound to put a different complexion upon things.'

'You must convince Lady Catherine of that,' Davidson said. 'I'm ready to accept my dismissal, but you must forgive me if I decline to do anything to facilitate it. On the contrary, I'll insist upon seeing Lady Catherine before she absolutely decides. I'll not plead with her - you need not be afraid of that - but I'll want to be quite sure that there has been no misunderstanding of any sort.'

'There is no time like the present,' Sir Andrew Linton said. 'Drive home with me, and we will interview my daughter at once.'

She heard all that her father had to say, listened to him gravely and attentively. Then she turned to Davidson. 'And you?' she said. 'What do you say to it all?'

'My dear Catherine,' Davidson said, 'it amounts to this. I'm to be the hero or victim, as the case may be, of a cause célèbre. I cannot come out of it with any considerable credit; I may come out to find myself under very grave suspicion. I admit that appearances are against me. There will even be people who will whisper that I sent Haynes from my office as an assassin to Austin, and that the deed he brought with him from South Africa is in my safe, or at the back of my fire. No one has ever been free from calumny. I certainly am going to have my share of it. It may - it very likely will - lessen my prestige. You will find some of your friends who will talk of the 'Davidson Blackmailing Affair,' and who will never be quite sure whether I was prosecutor or defendant. You will find all your life my name looked upon with a certain amount of suspicion, because, in a case of this sort, prosecutor and defendant, and even the witnesses, are all classed together by that somewhat vague portion of the public which your friends represent. I admit all this. I also admit that it would be an act of perfect justice if you should tell me to kiss your hands and go.'

She pointed to the door. 'Father,' she said, 'will you leave us for a moment? There is something which I have to say to Malcolm.'

Chapter 31

Even after the door had closed upon Sir Andrew Linton, and Davidson was alone with his fiancée, words did not seem to come easily to either of them. Lady Catherine was sitting back in the corner of a low couch. Davidson was standing upon the hearthrug, his hands behind him, his face a little wrinkled with perplexity.

'I suppose,' he said thoughtfully, 'you would like me, Catherine, to explain exactly how this claim came about?'

'On the contrary,' she said, 'I do not wish you to do anything of the sort.'

He looked at her in some surprise. Her voice had prepared him for a change of some sort, but he was nevertheless puzzled. There was a slight flush of colour in her cheeks, and her eyes were softer than usual.

'Malcolm,' she said, 'come and sit down here by my side.'

He obeyed at once. She turned and faced him.

'I'm puzzled, Malcolm,' she said. 'I want to ask you a question. You have been lunching with my father?'

'Yes!' Davidson said. 'At his club.'

'I know that he feels very strongly about this matter,' she said. 'Tell me, did the suggestion that our engagement should be broken off come from him?'

'Certainly.'

'And you?' she said. 'Tell me exactly what you felt, what it meant to you? I don't want you to fence with words, please,' she went on. 'Tell me this honestly. Was it anything of a relief to you?'

'Assuredly not,' he said wonderingly.

'Think again,' she begged. 'You answer quickly, but is that because you are very, very sure, or because you are taking it for granted? You see you are one of those men, Malcolm,' she went on earnestly, 'whose disposition does not allow them to look back. We are engaged, I was your deliberate choice, and after that, so far as you are concerned, the matter was ended. The possibility that you had made a mistake would never occur to you, simply because you would regard the matter as inevitable. Tell me, if it were not inevitable, if you were not engaged to me at this moment, Malcolm, would you ask me again?'

Her words amazed him. He had never given her credit for such insight, such perceptions. It seemed, indeed, as though she had realized something of which he himself was not yet conscious, and yet something which might very well exist.

'How long have you had this idea, Catherine?' he said gravely.

'All the time,' she said. 'At first, of course, it seemed all right, but up in Scotland, and since then, I have wondered whether you have not looked upon me as something quite outside your life, - a necessary and desirable adjunct, perhaps, to your household and growing prosperity. Don't think that I'm complaining,' she continued, 'but in all our recent communications the personal note has not been very strongly marked, has it? I can see exactly, too, how my father's suggestion has moved you. You don't feel, do you, as though the sun had ceased to shine, or the world to move, because there is a chance that you may lose me?'

Davidson was not often so doubtful of himself. In a sense he knew that she was right. And yet, her very apprehension of these things, the new earnestness with which she was looking at him, the thought that he was very near indeed to losing her, seemed to stimulate his interest, - made him feel, indeed, that it would not be a light thing to give her up.

'Catherine,' he said, 'I wish I could make you know exactly how I feel. If I have been a little slow and reticent of speech, believe me, it is not that I have not cared. On the other hand, there is some truth in what you have said - I mean that I do honestly believe that I have taken things a little too much for granted, that knowing there was no other woman in my life, knowing how desirable you were, and how really fond of you I was, I think I was content to let the rest come, as I certainly did feel that it would come.'

'I think I understand,' she said slowly. 'Now tell me exactly what you think of my father's request?'

'I think that it is reasonable,' Davidson said. 'It is more reasonable, even, than your father knows of. I think that I have been a little too successful, perhaps, during these later years of my life. I have grown to underestimate the possibilities of trouble.'

'This is really serious, then?'

He nodded. 'I'm afraid,' he said, 'that I've been a little over-bold. I ought to have kicked that man van Heerden out of my office half-a-dozen times, until he came to reason, and then bought him off for good for a thousand pounds. But you see I didn't. All my life I have hated compromises. I knew that he was a blackguard, and I dealt with him as a blackguard, and I've left him with the cards in his hands.'

'Then I suppose my father was right,' she said, sighing.

'I suppose he was,' Davidson said.

She held out her hand. 'Very well, Malcolm,' she said, 'let it be so. Our engagement is broken. See that the proper steps are taken to announce it. But I want you to understand this from me, that if you had cared, if I could have seen any signs whatever of your caring, no word of my father's, nor anything that could have happened to you in the city or elsewhere, any disgrace or any loss of money, could have separated us.'

He took a step towards her. 'Catherine!' he said

'No!' she said, a little sharply, and rang the bell.

He turned and walked out. In the hall he passed Sir Andrew Linton. 'We have arranged it according to your wish, sir,' he said, 'your daughter and I.'

Sir Andrew Linton looked at him curiously. Davidson had the look of a man who has been hard hit.

'I'm sorry, Davidson. I hope you understand there's nothing personal in it.'

'I understand!' Davidson said, briefly.

Chapter 32

From the pit of the world - from the Law Courts, hot and crowded, where the atmosphere was heavy with strife, - the modern battleground, where the fighting was at least as dramatic over the souls of men as on those other fields, reddened with their blood, Davidson escaped to find himself, after a few hours' journey, in this strangest of churchyards upon the bare hillside. The church itself, squat, square-towered, and tumbling into decay, stood out like a watch-tower upon the cliff. The churchyard, bordered by low grey stone walls, seemed to contain little more than a dozen or so of graves, and from one of these Davidson turned away, and with Eileen by his side started the long descent to the level of the sea. The half-a-dozen who had attended the ceremony out of curiosity had already melted away. The parson, with his book under his arm, had gone into the vestry, but neither custom nor age had failed to rob those few sentences of their wonderful, threatening pathos. Even Davidson was a little moved. The girl who walked by his side carried still with her that impenetrable mask, but there was something more like real sadness in the steady gaze of her unseeing eyes.

The air was filled with sunshine, the singing of larks, and the calling of the white-winged seagulls wheeling about their heads. Below, the sea had receded to its furthest limits. The creeks were dry. The shore was piled with masses of fragrant seaweed. The grass-grown dykes which led down to the tower stood high and dry, like ribbons across the land. Little sandy spits were visible, far out from the shore, and only the white-topped posts marked the way of the tidal river out beyond the island of seagulls and sand.

Davidson, after his anxious days and his tearing ride from town in the great motor, felt the peace of all these things, showed it in his face, felt it in his heart. The last few days had taught him a good deal. Never had he been so weary of his place in the great world as he was that afternoon. Even that little ceremony in the wind-swept churchyard, the coffin lowered into the grave, the heaping of earth, the simple words spoken by the bareheaded vicar, - even that little ceremony had left its impression. After all, how small the difference between Death and Life. His own reputation had many times during the last few days trembled in the balance. What was the value of that, even, - of all his wealth, - compared to the great primeval facts of life?

His thoughts suddenly turned to the girl by his side. He looked at her pityingly, - looked at her, too, with curiosity. She had accepted his coming almost as a matter of course. All the time, though he had known well that she was suffering, she had been wordless, as though her grief were something so great that no outward sign of it could be anything else but pitifully inadequate. In her quiet, graceful walk, the very reserve, the negativeness, so to speak, of her colouring, her speech, her looks, she still represented to him an insoluble enigma. Was it possible, now that her brother had gone, that she would speak? In any case, the silence between them could not continue much longer, for already they were down on the marshes, and, as though by common consent, had turned seaward, towards where the lonely grey tower stood out on its little sandy eminence.

'Tell me, Miss Haynes,' he said, 'what are your plans now?'

'My plans?' she repeated, without turning her head.

'Yes!' he went on. 'I know that your brother's death is a blow to you, but remember that it was inevitable. It was a thing which was bound to come, and in many ways it was kinder and better that it should happen like this. You could not have chosen for him a more peaceful ending, a more peaceful resting-place. For anyone with even the faintest beliefs in the future life could anything be more beautiful than to rest there, with the eternal lullaby of the sea in his ears, free from encroachment, save the encroachment of nature herself?'

She turned to look at him, and the calm scrutiny of her level grey eyes somehow disturbed him. 'It is easy for you to talk like that,' she said. 'You are still young and strong, and if the pendulum of fate swings against you one day, it pays you back the next. You are selfish because you cannot help it. You cannot even realize the hideousness of death! You cannot realize it because it comes to other people, and not to you!'

'You are a little unfair, Miss Haynes,' Davidson said. 'You must remember that your brother was a doomed man.'

'Yes, but why?' she cried. 'He was younger than you. There were no worse things in his life. Always he was battling with failure and disappointment. And this is the end, - to sit opposite a doctor, and be told you may live a month, three months, a measure of time. Oh! it's easy to think about it for other people! Think of yourself going about with the knowledge in your heart that as the days passed one by one they brought you nearer to the end, that every morning when your eyes opened, instead of the joy of life would come once more that terrible fear.'

'Your brother was not a coward, Miss Haynes,' Davidson said.

'A coward! You mean that he did not show his sufferings!' she said 'That does not mean that he did not suffer. Oh! I have heard him in the night when he thought that he was alone, I have heard his agony. And that is the end!'

She turned and faced the little stone church on the hill, the rudely enclosed churchyard, in the far corner of which was still visible the bare heap of mould.

'He felt it coming, he felt the strength pass from him day by day, - he, who had never known what it was to live, who had never known the days of riches or success or power. There he lies, - God knows for what purpose, to what end!'

Davidson walked for a little way in silence. It seemed to him that the girl's bitterness was scarcely reasonable. Yet he realized that at such a time reason loses its power.

'His last days, at least, were as comfortable as possible.'

'Comfortable!' she exclaimed scornfully. 'He lived in hell!'

'You are not blaming me, by any chance?' Davidson said quietly.

She turned upon him, and the mask seemed suddenly raised. There blazed into her eyes a great fire. There trembled in the notes of her voice a wonderful passion. Her form seemed to dilate. They were walking now upon the top of the dyke, and she seemed to have been suddenly transformed into something vengeful, some grim representation of Fate.

'Blame you!' she cried. 'I tell you that I hate all you smug, successful, phrase-making men, who succeeded where he failed. What are you that he was not? He was brave, he worked hard, he was honest, courageous, he was all that a man should be. If you were ever these things you at least were not more, and to you comes wealth and easy days, honour, a long, peaceful future. London - the world - is full of you, grubbing your way through life, thinking what magnificent creatures you are, opening your pockets to help with your alms those who have fallen, those who, if there was justice upon the earth, should be in your places!'

'This is unreasonable,' Davidson said coldly.

'Unreasonable! Who said it was anything else?' she cried. 'What reason is there in life, in death, in success or failure? Can you tell me the laws by which life is ruled, can you find them anywhere, at the base of any man's success or another's failure? Reasonable, indeed! One man swims and another drowns. Who can tell why? One man grows rich, another starves, and as often as not it is the clever man who starves and the fool who grows rich. There is no reason in those things. There is no reason in my hate for you and all those who have lived easy lives, and who go on living them while he - lies there!'

She turned back once more and pointed with outstretched hand towards the little church. The wind blew her skirts about her, - disturbed for once the trim, uncompromising arrangement of her hair. The colour had come into her cheeks at last. Davidson wondered why he had never before thought her beautiful!

'I'm sorry you are feeling like this,' he said. 'I did what I could for your brother.'

'Be silent!' she interrupted fiercely. 'You did what you could! To insure your own safety you sent him on a desperate, unworthy mission - to worm his way into the confidence of a drunkard, to steal for you, to be your jackal. What did you care what the consequences might be! What did you care, so long as your own reputation and wealth were saved! He was to be one other - my poor Brian - one other of those to be crushed beneath the great wheels!'

'It is not fair,' replied Davidson, 'to make such statements. Your brother knew his risks, and he took them.'

'Knew his risks!' she repeated. 'You mean that because you were on your feet when he was on the ground, you would make use of him like any other lump of mud you would spurn with your foot if you had not found a use for it. He did your bidding, poor fool, but where he failed, I succeeded. You have to deal with me now, and I think that it is my turn to make terms!'

Davidson looked at her curiously. 'At last,' he said, 'you are going to admit your possession of that little document?'

'At last,' she admitted, 'I'm going to tell you that I have it!'

'And to name your price?' he said.

There was a queer little sound in her throat, like an unnatural laugh. 'My price! Yes, that is another matter!'

Chapter 33

Southward, through the country lanes whose hedges were still wreathed with late honeysuckle, on to the great main road, Davidson's car was driven through the night, - always southward, till the lights of the great city flared before them up into the sky. Davidson himself, for hour after hour, had sat back in his corner, buried in thought. His companion was even more invisible, but as the end of the journey drew near he roused himself with an effort, looked into the half-hidden face of the girl who was reclining by his side.

'My dearest,' he said, 'we are nearing London. Won't you rouse yourself and give me your further orders?'

She sat up, with a little yawn. 'Let down the windows, please,' she said'

He obeyed her at once. The sweet midnight air through which they were rushing was like a douche of cold water upon her face.

'How far are we from London?' she said.

'Less than twenty miles. Unless we are stopped, we shall certainly be there in half-an-hour.'

'Why did you disturb me?' she said.

'To know your wishes.'

'You had better leave me at one of the small hotels in the west end,' she said. 'I dare say you can think of one at which you are known. In the morning, please come and see me and bring some money. I'll want to engage a companion and a maid, and to buy some clothes.'

Davidson looked at her curiously. Her manner was perfectly natural. 'Anything else?' he said calmly.

'I don't think so,' she said.

'You mentioned the fact, I believe,' he continued, 'that you were - that you had done me the honour - that you were, in fact, my fiancée.'

'Well?' she said.

'Under those circumstances,' he continued, 'don't you think -'

His hand rested for a moment upon hers. She drew it at once away. 'No, I think not!' she said.

'I have not had much experience,' he went on, 'in being engaged, but it seemed to me that there were certain privileges which belonged to that state.'

'You are perfectly well aware,' she said, 'that ours is not an engagement of that sort. You know something about the world in which the men marry for position and the women for money, don't you? You can look upon our engagement as being of that order. I marry you because it is the only way I can make you pay your debt. I have given you notice from the first. I mean to gain everything I can, and to give nothing.'

'Nothing?' he repeated.

'As little as possible,' she said. 'As a matter of fact, you are singularly indifferent to me. You simply represent the things I desire, the things which are owing to me, the things which were owing to - to him. I marry you to acquire them. You marry me because you must.'

'Well,' he said, 'ours promises to be a novel matrimonial experience.'

'Then we,' she said, 'will remain exceptions.'

'Do you dislike me?' he said.

'Personally I have not thought about you,' she said. 'Apart from that, I hate you. You represent the victor, and all that I have loved upon this earth have been the vanquished. Willingly I would not give you so much as the touch of my fingers. If I thought that my presence was a pleasure to you, I would shrink back into myself. If I thought that any happiness could come to you from our association, even now I would throw myself from the car and end it.'

'Our prospects of matrimonial bliss,' he said, 'appear to me to be distinctly above the average.'

'I do not expect,' she said, 'to find any pleasure that may come to me in later life, at your hands.'

'I'll certainly not allow you to flirt.'

'I know the law,' she said. 'I know what I may do and what I may not do. I'll not transgress it. I want your money, I want your position, I want your power. These things I will share with you. For the rest, you cannot keep too far away to please me.'

He leaned towards her, heedless of the fact that she was shrinking away. There was something a little pitiful in the blue-grey eyes which tried so hard to hold him at a distance. 'Well,' said he, 'it will be an interesting experiment, at any rate. Personally, I think that you are a brave woman. I wonder that you did not take the money without me.'

'What good would that have been to me?' she said. 'I have no name, no friends. Can't you imagine the sort of people who would have come hanging on to my skirts, if I had made my début on the scene as a widow or a spinster with a large fortune, unattached, looking for companions? No! I need your name, Mr. Malcolm Davidson.'

'I'm not at all sure,' he said grimly, 'that you will find that much of an asset.'

'You must see to it that I do find it an asset, and a valuable one,' she said. 'You are relieved now from any fear of that deed being produced. There is no shadow of evidence to connect you with the man Austin, or with my brother's transaction with him. If your lawyers are clever and you are brave, you must win your case with honour, and van Heerden will be sent to prison. He deserves it, in any case.'

Davidson nodded. 'I'll win my case all right,' he said. 'For me there never was any danger except in the production of that document, concerning which you have been so mysterious.'

'It was mine,' she said. 'I ran all the risk to get it. I ran risks the memory of which will haunt me all my days. I have lost Brian. All that I can do is to exact the utmost price that you can pay for that little paper.'

'It isn't worth it, you know,' Davidson said. 'I believe, even now, that I'd win my case.'

She smiled - a curious little contraction of the corners of her lips. Her eyes mocked him. 'Perhaps,' she said, 'but it is a different thing since Austin's murder. Its production today would ruin you inevitably, whether it were held a legal document or not.'

'We all make mistakes,' he said, looking out of the window.

'But too often others pay for them!' she said, turning away.

Presently he gave some instructions to the chauffeur. The pace of the car slackened as they reached the outskirts of London and turned westward.

'Well,' he said, 'the world is full of surprises for us. I little thought, when I came down here, that it was to find a bride!'

She shivered a little at his words, but made no reply.

'Forgive me,' he said, 'if I don't seem very coherent about it all. As a matter of fact, you see, I was not expecting to take up obligations of this sort again so quickly.'

'If you don't mind,' she said coldly, 'we will not discuss it.'

'I may at least be permitted to ask,' he continued, 'when it is your intention to - marry me?'

'In about two months' time,' she said.

'You would like our engagement announced?' he said.

She hesitated for a few seconds. 'In a fortnight's time,' she said.

'In the meantime?' he inquired.

'I'll expect to lunch and dine with you occasionally, to be taken to the theatres, and for short expeditions into the country.'

'Delightful!'

The car stopped at one of the smallest and most famous of semi-private hotels, in the neighbourhood of Bond Street.

'If you will come in for a moment,' he said, 'I will arrange things for you here. They know me very well.'

She followed him into the hotel and waited while he interviewed the manager. Then he took his leave of her, bowing over her reluctantly offered hand, and smiling into her face as though honestly anxious to penetrate behind its absolute imperturbability.

'I hope you will find the little suite comfortable,' he said. 'You must go to bed soon, and try and rest. They will do everything that is possible for you, I'm sure. Good-night!'

She raised her eyes for a moment to his, but there was more indignation than gratitude in the glance she threw upon him. 'I'm very much obliged to you. Good-night!'

Davidson drove back to his rooms. As yet he could scarcely realize the situation. Had anyone ever been confronted with a position so unique? The mystery of the girl's impenetrability was solved at last!

Chapter 34

The curtain had fallen upon the first act of this little drama in Davidson's life. Van Heerden was committed for trial. Davidson had walked into the court a few minutes late, as though the whole affair was one which interested him only indirectly. He had gone into the witness box without hesitation, and his story had been so perfectly rational and straightforward that people began to wonder whether, indeed, any defence was possible. Cross-examination only amused him. Van Heerden, who went into court expecting to be released, was committed at once to the Old Bailey, and to everyone's surprise, his own included, was refused bail.

Davidson left the court a few minutes after the case was closed, and paused for a moment on the steps. On the edge of the pavement there was a woman who watched with steady and scrutinizing interest every person who left the entrance of the Law Courts. When Davidson came out she advanced towards him. 'Is van Heerden free?' she said.

Davidson looked at her, and recognized at once Hannah Austin.

'No!' he said. 'He is committed for trial.'

'You -'

She leaned forward as though about to strike him. Davidson neither shrank back nor showed any sign of interest in her words.

'What is van Heerden to you?' he said quickly.

'He is no blackmailer, at any rate!' she said fiercely.

'The Court has ventured to think otherwise,' Davidson said.

She was almost at his side now. Suddenly his eyes caught the sight of something glittering, something half drawn from the pocket of her dress. Her wrist was caught in a clasp of iron.

'Young lady,' he said sternly, 'are you mad?'

'If I'm, it is your fault,' she said.

'Nonsense!' he said. 'You see that policeman there? He is watching us now. Let go the revolver and be off. I don't want to give you into custody - my life is worth something for others as well as myself - and I'll certainly do it unless you obey me.'

She gave a little sob, and her fingers relaxed their hold upon the revolver, which Davidson transferred into his own pocket. She glided away into the crowd. Davidson stepped into his taxi, giving the man the address of the hotel where Eileen Haynes was staying. He leaned back in the seat, looking at the little weapon in his hands. Somehow, the fact of his escape, instead of bringing any exultation with it, seemed to depress him strangely. Davidson had never called himself or believed himself to be a religious man, yet there was certainly one principle which had always been part of his creed, - to live and let live. He was not a greedy capitalist. He could look upon money without any desire to absorb it. Yet lately he seemed to have been forced into tortuous paths. From the moment when he had attempted to make use of Haynes as a tool, everything had gone against him. Haynes himself lay dead in that windy churchyard, and the words which had been spoken over Haynes's grave were still fresh in his memory. He had lost Catherine, of whom, in a way, he had been fond. And at her own bidding he was engaged to this strange, impenetrable girl, a situation which he could not wholly realize, and yet which he felt to be surrounded with danger and humiliation. Then there was this other, - Hannah Austin, - who had come to London expecting to find a fortune, and had found nothing but her uncle's dead body. She, too, looked upon him as a hungry schemer, the indirect cause of her uncle's death, a robber, if not a murderer! He looked at the little revolver, opened it carelessly, and laughed as he stared into the empty breech. It was unloaded, a brand-new toy which had never been discharged. He threw it into the opposite seat with a little gesture of contempt. All its tragedy seemed to have passed away. She had bought it to frighten him with. There had, after all, been no serious purpose in her mind. She too, perhaps, had hoped to play the part of extortioner.

What was his offence, he said himself, as his taxi glided along the Embankment. Simply this: there had been a claim presented for his mine, which was, without doubt, a fraud, which few people would ever have believed in, and which, in a court of law, would have stood but little chance of success. What a fool he had been not to defy Austin, to go to his directors and tell them the truth, to resist stoutly any claim the man might bring! Since his first compromise with Haynes, everything had gone wrong. It was unworthy for a man in his position to have allowed Haynes even to play the ambassador, apart from anything else. He saw very clearly in those few minutes where the mistake of his life had been. What he could not see was whither he was tending.

Eileen was waiting for him in the hall of the small hotel in Dover Street. For three days, at her own request, he had not seen her. Nothing, however, had prepared him for the transformation which he now saw. She was faultlessly dressed in a gown of the latest design, and a picture hat which even he recognized as being something quite apart from the usual efforts of even the Bond Street shopkeepers. In every detail she seemed to express the wholly self-satisfied, half-insolent perfection of the woman who knows that she may and does command the best of everything. And with this change in her dress seemed to have come a similar change in her deportment. Her aloofness was still evident enough, but she carried herself with confidence, and with a sort of languid, graceful ease.

'You are nearly ten minutes late,' she said quietly. 'Where are you taking me to lunch?'

'Wherever you like,' he said. 'What about Prince's?'

She took a gold purse and a tiny black spaniel from the neatly dressed maid who stood by her side, and lifting her skirts in her other hand, passed through the door which he was holding open. The lace of her petticoat, the slenderness of her arched instep, the delicate narrowness of her patent shoes, were revelations to him. He gave an order to his chauffeur, and sat down by her side.

'You appear,' he said, 'to possess a gift for assimilation!'

'My sex is like that,' she said. 'I have had a good many years to wait, to store up knowledge in. Besides,' she continued, a little mockingly, 'you yourself are supposed to be something exceptional in the way of grooming, aren't you? There is no need for other people to find our engagement surprising.'

Looking at her critically, 'I think,' he said, 'that there is no fear of that.'

'You flatter me,' she said.

'Not at all,' he said. 'People might wonder, perhaps, how it is possible to fall in love with anyone whose expression so much resembles that of those statues in there,' pointing to a gallery which they were passing. 'You have no other fault. There is none, at least, to be found in your appearance. You certainly do look, however, a little inclined to be faultily faultless.'

She laughed, - a laugh, however, which brought no colour into her cheeks or light into her eyes. 'I'm a statue,' she said, 'into which life has not yet been breathed. You see you have been a little remiss up till now. You have never attempted to make love to me!'

'Do you mean to say - ' he said, leaning towards her, -

She gently pushed back his hand, saying: 'Please don't be ridiculous. Of course, you must know that overtures of that sort, under the circumstances, are impossible.'

'For always?' he said.

'Certainly!'

'Perhaps you will draw up a little code of conditions,' he said. 'I feel a little in the dark sometimes as to what is expected of me.'

'You will easily pick it up as we go along,' she replied. 'Is this Prince's? I wonder if I'll succeed in behaving as though I had lunched here every day of my life!'

Chapter 35

Davidson found a singular interest, an interest which amounted almost to fascination, in watching the demeanour and general deportment of his companion. Her adaptability was little short of marvellous. She smiled at the right moment at the obsequious maître d'hôtel, and exhibited just the proper amount of interest in the luncheon which Davidson ordered. The restaurant was somewhat crowded, but there was no one who attracted more notice than Davidson and the girl who sat opposite him, - slim, and elegantly dressed, - looking around her with a certain partly veiled interest, which was all the time in piquant contrast to the languor of her eyes and manner. She was by no means a silent companion, although her conversation consisted for the most part of questions. She had an unerring gift for discovering the most noteworthy of the little crowd by whom they were surrounded, and she was continually asking questions about them, with a persistence which clearly indicated an interest scarcely suggested by her general deportment.

'I wonder,' Davidson said, toward the end of their meal, 'whether social pre-eminence is amongst your carefully veiled ambitions.'

'I'm not at all sure,' she said. 'Of course, one develops according to circumstances. In the office I naturally cared nothing for the world which I could only read about in the columns of Vogue. As one comes into touch with things, one appreciates. It is always interesting to know people.'

'I'm afraid,' Davidson said, 'that my friends are scarcely what you would call fashionable.'

'Your friends?' she said, looking up at him. 'But that doesn't matter, does it? I'll make my own friends later on.'

Davidson looked across the table. She was patting the head of her little spaniel, and watching, with a self-possession which amounted almost to insolence, the exodus of a party from the neighbouring table.

'Young lady,' he said, 'what sort of a life did you lead before? I always understood that your people were very poor, and only respectably connected.'

'You understood the truth,' she said, with composure.

'Will you tell me, then,' he said, 'how you learned to wear your clothes? - how you picked up all the little tricks of the high life?'

The very faintest of smiles parted her lips, a smile that wrinkled at the corners of her eyes, and suddenly altered her appearance so that Davidson was forced to recognize the charm which even to himself he had denied.

'My dear Mr. Davidson,' she said, 'it is the natural heritage of a woman to assimilate quickly, especially,' she added, after a moment's pause, 'amongst surroundings for which she has had a great desire. Many a time when I was typing price-lists in that wretched little office, in a black alpaca gown, with my hat hanging up opposite me, - a black straw with faded flowers, which had cost me three or four shillings, with darned stockings and patched boots, - many a time I have left off typing for a few minutes, and thought and wondered what this must be like. I suppose I have what you would call a natural aptitude for it. It is because I have thought of it, pondered over it, desired it.'

Davidson looked at her wonderingly.

'Well,' he said, 'let me congratulate you. You play the game to perfection. If I were in a position to make terms -'

'You are not,' she interrupted shortly. 'Please pay the bill. I'm going to take you shopping.'

They left the taxi at the corner of Bond Street. Eileen had signified her desire to walk for a little time. Davidson found himself becoming thoroughly interested - not, as he told himself, in his companion herself, but in his study of her. The women they passed she subjected, nearly every one of them, to a close and comprehensive scrutiny. At the men she scarcely glanced. She found, perhaps, her greatest interest in the shop windows. She led him across the road to the establishment of a great jeweller.

'You have not given me an engagement ring,' she said, a little abruptly. 'Shall we go in and choose one.'

He followed her obediently into the shop, and stood by her side while she described minutely the sort of ring she required. Her manner inspired instant respect. She knew exactly what she wanted, and what she wanted was the rarest and most beautiful stones, set in the newest fashion. She showed very little enthusiasm - hesitated, even - over the ring which was produced at last, after a little hesitation, and shown almost with reverence. It had been made for a queen, but something had gone wrong - a matter of politics - and they had not dared to part with it. Even Davidson stared when the man at his elbow whispered the price, but Eileen never moved a muscle.

'I think it will do,' she said, turning to him. 'It is very nearly what I wanted. And I want a few pins - emeralds and diamonds I prefer.'

The shop man was already producing a tray from the window. She spoke of pearls, and examined those that were shown her with the air of a connoisseur.

'I'll want a rope of pearls very soon,' she told the man, 'but not just yet. Perhaps you will let Mr. Davidson know when you have enough of the ones the colour and size I like.'

'It will give us very great pleasure, madam, to collect them,' the man said, bowing.

Davidson produced his cheque-book - fortunately, he was well known - and wrote a cheque for over two thousand pounds in exchange for the receipt which the man handed to him. Eileen calmly withdrew her glove and slipped on the ring. The other things she said them to send. When she left the shop, it seemed to Davidson that there was a little more colour in her cheeks and a deeper light in her eyes.

'Jewellery interests you?' he said, as they stood for a moment on the pavement.

'Yes!' she said. 'Of course it does. Everything of this sort interests me. Haven't I longed all my days to feel the touch of pearls upon my bare neck, to have something like this upon my finger that I could look at and worship, not only for itself but for the things it represents? Come and buy me some flowers. My sitting-room is a wilderness. Afterwards, I'm going into the milliner's beyond.'

Davidson followed her obediently into the florist's opposite. She chose a great bowl of pink roses and some white lilac.

'How many of the roses, madam?' the man said.

She looked at him with faintly upraised eyebrows. 'Oh! send them as they are,' she said.

'There are four dozen, madam.'

She nodded indifferently.

'Is that all the lilacs you have?' she said, as they were leaving the shop.

'All we have at present, madam,' the man said.

'Please get some more,' she said, 'if you can. These hotel sitting-rooms,' she added, turning to Davidson, 'seem to have a sort of odour all their own. One can only get rid of it by having flowers everywhere. Now I'm going in here,' she said, stopping at a milliner's. 'You must wait for me. Do you have money?'

'I'm afraid,' Davidson said, 'I have only twenty pounds with me. But I'll soon get more.'

She nodded, and disappeared into the shop. When she came out again, she was all smiles.

'We can perhaps continue our shopping,' Davidson said, 'more comfortably now.'

She ignored the faint note of satire in his tone.

'One needs so many things,' she said. 'The woman inside is just making out my bill. I think I'll want another -.'

'Whatever it takes,' Davidson said.

She turned back into the shop, and he followed her. A lace dressing-gown was lying upon a chair, and in a few moments Davidson found it being held up before him by a vivacious shop assistant who was endeavouring to convince him that in it Madame would look a dream. It was very filmy, very dainty, and damned expensive. Davidson heard the price without so much as the twitch of a muscle.

'I think you'd better have it,' he said. 'I'm sure you'll look lovely in it.'

Once more they were in the street.

'I want a new handbag,' she said, a little abruptly.

'By all means,' he said. 'Louis Vuitton be all right?"

'I'm not sure,' she said. 'I'd like to look at some.'

They were twenty minutes or so making a selection. Davidson again used his Mastercard and stuffed another receipt into his pocket.

'Where to now?' he said.

'I want some gloves,' she said. 'Perhaps you would rather go back to your office now. I mustn't take up your whole afternoon.'

'I'm entirely at your service,' he assured her. 'I find shopping quite an interesting novelty.'

'You mean,' she said, 'that you like to watch the effect upon me. You think I don't understand. It's quite easy. Tell me how I seem to you?'

'You seem very much to the manner born,' he said, 'but you seem also, if I may say so, as though you were getting rid of the pent-up desires of years. I'm not complaining,' he added quickly. 'As a matter of fact, I'm rather inclined to welcome any note of humanity. So long as we're engaged,' he said, looking at her sideways, 'one would just as soon feel that one were engaged to a living person as an automaton.'

She kept her eyes averted, but he saw the colour burning in her cheeks.

Chapter 36

A man in the city, who was an old friend of Sir Andrew Linton, stopped the latter as he was on the point of entering his club.

'By the bye, Linton,' he said, 'did I understand - I think I saw it in the papers - that the marriage between your daughter and Malcolm Davidson was off?'

'The engagement has been broken off,' said Sir Andrew Linton, a little stiffly. 'Why?'

'That's all right,' said the man. 'The only thing was that as I was one of the people you came to, to ask about Davidson, I felt that if it was still on I ought to tell you that things aren't supposed to be just the same as they were.'

'Do you mean about Davidson?' said Sir Andrew Linton.

His friend nodded. 'There are some very curious rumours going about,' he said. 'You remember, of course, his charging a man named van Heerden - a South African - with an attempt at blackmail the other day? The man was committed for trial, and there was not much came out in the evidence before the magistrates. Since then, however, people have been talking. They say that van Heerden had actual knowledge of documents proving that Davidson's title to the Letlakana Mine was a false one, and that the mine in reality belonged to van Heerden himself and a partner.'

'That sounds like a very curious story,' Sir Andrew Linton said. 'If it is true, why doesn't van Heerden produce his document and have done with it?'

'Because it has been stolen,' the other said. 'There are all sorts of stories going about, too, concerning the theft. The point remains, however, that there is a strong feeling that the document in question does exist, and that it may turn up. If so, of course, it would ruin Davidson. I see that the shares of his corporation have had a most tremendous drop, so it seems as though there might be something in it. Buy a special edition this afternoon, and you'll know more about it.'

Sir Andrew Linton nodded. 'Thank you,' he said, 'I will do so.'

Sir Andrew Linton walked slowly along Pall Mall. After all, there was no need to buy a paper. On the placards which the boys were displaying as he neared Trafalgar Square were great headlines, -

Extraordinary Drop of Shares in the Mines Association. Panic in the City.

Sir Andrew Linton bought a paper, and stood for a few minutes reading it. Then he called a taxicab, and gave the man the address of Davidson's offices. He was well known there, and Davidson's confidential man at once came forward.

'Mr. Davidson will see you, of course, my lord,' he said. 'He is really disengaged now, but we are obliged to deny him to everybody because of these interviewers. Will you come with me, my lord?'

Sir Andrew Linton found himself ushered into Davidson's private room. Davidson was dictating rapidly to his secretary. As usual he was calm, self-possessed, carefully groomed and dressed. There was nothing about his appearance in any way to suggest a panic. He heard his visitor's name, however, with surprise.

'Linton!' he exclaimed, rising to his feet.

Sir Andrew Linton nodded, and held out his hand. 'I was in the city and thought I'd look you up, Davidson,' he said. 'Can I have a word or two with you?'

'Certainly,' Davidson said. 'Give us five minutes, Ellison, - or stay away until I ring,' he added to his secretary.

Sir Andrew Linton accepted an easy-chair but he seemed in no great hurry to explain his business. 'I was very sorry, Malcolm,' he said at last, 'to see the papers this evening. I hope the trouble isn't very serious.'

'Do you hold any of our shares?' Davidson said.

'If I did,' said the other, colouring a little, 'I'd not have come here.'

Davidson accepted the reproof. 'I beg your pardon.'

'I dare say,' continued Sir Andrew Linton, 'my coming seems to you, under the circumstances, a little superfluous. However, what I wanted to say is this. You see Catherine is our only child, and that made us very anxious about anything to do with her. I'm sure that you yourself must feel now, when you are under so much anxiety, that it is better not to have the added responsibility of your engagement upon your shoulders.'

'I have never questioned your wisdom in breaking it off,' Davidson said quietly. 'Under the circumstances, I agree with you that it is a very good thing.'

'That's all right,' Sir Andrew Linton continued, a little hastily. 'Of course, neither you nor Catherine are children, and you are not the sort to wear your hearts upon your sleeve. In short,' he added, somewhat abruptly, 'you'll both get over it. There's no doubt about that. I didn't come to revert to this matter at all. I simply wanted to say that though our relations are changed, I still do feel a considerable amount of friendship for you, Davidson, and I wanted to come and just tell you I was sorry. And look here,' he went on, a little awkwardly, 'I've between seven and eight thousand pounds for which I'm looking for an investment, and if the money's any use to you, Davidson, why say the word, and I'll write you a cheque on the spot.'

Davidson looked at his visitor for a moment in an astonishment which triumphed over the natural impassivity of his expression. Then a little flush rose in his cheeks. He got to his feet and held out his hand.

'Linton,' he said, 'this is awfully good of you. I'll not forget it. Believe that. If we wanted money, or if I did personally, I'd accept your offer like a shot.'

'Too much of a drop in the bucket, I suppose,' Sir Andrew Linton said. 'It isn't much, I know.'

'It isn't that,' Davidson interrupted. 'The situation is simply that our shares have had a big drop because of rumours concerning our title to the Letlakana Mine. If those rumours were confirmed - If they are not confirmed, and if they die a natural death, as I imagine they must, our shares will recover themselves and we shall not need money.'

'You don't believe in the existence of any such document, then?' Sir Andrew Linton said.

'I don't believe that it will be produced,' Davidson said, 'and if it were produced,' he went on, 'I do not believe in its validity. I would not say as much, even, as this to the reporters, but the document about which people have been talking is simply an original claim to the Letlakana Mine, which was deserted by the very man who put me on to it, and in whose name the claim stands. You see, therefore, that any attempt to establish a legal claim is more or less a swindle.'

Sir Andrew Linton rose to his feet. 'You are really not so very much alarmed, then?'

Davidson shook his head. 'This drop in shares, after all,' he said, 'does not affect us particularly, except for the time. It simply means that the market declares that we are a few hundred thousand pounds poorer today than we were yesterday. Whether the market is right or not remains to be proved.'

'Well, I'm glad to have seen you, at any rate, Malcolm, and remember, if there's anything I can do -'

'You have already,' Davidson said, 'done a great deal, Sir Andrew Linton. I'll not forget your visit or your offer.'

'That's all right,' Sir Andrew Linton said. 'Catherine didn't know I was coming, but I'm sure if she had. She would have sent her love. Don't bother to ring. I can find my way out.'

The visit of his projected father-in-law seemed to Davidson like a pleasant little oasis in the middle of a long, dreary day. These rumours which Sir Andrew Linton had heard seemed to have come into existence during the last few hours. There had been some large failures lately, and investors were all nervous. The country was short of money. In ordinary times, an attack upon the stability of such a corporation as his would have been impossible. Today, nothing seemed impossible. In his heart, Davidson knew or felt that the situation was safe. Yet the very fact that rumours had sprung into being seemed to denote the line of defence which van Heerden's lawyers were prepared to offer in the coming trial. He would be accused everywhere - if not in words, in suggestion - of complicity in the murder of Austin. The existence of that document would be believed in. It would be said openly, perhaps, that he was responsible himself for its suppression. It was not the fact that on paper he was nearly a quarter of a million poorer than he had been a week ago that troubled him. It was the reflection that bold though his words had been, it was within the power of the man who lay awaiting his trial practically to ruin him. The question of the whereabouts of the document might be, in a few weeks, the most discussed matter in London.

Davidson, acting upon a sudden impulse, left his office by the back entrance and drove to the small hotel where Eileen was staying. Miss Haynes was at home, he was told, and after a few minutes' delay he was shown into her sitting-room.

'Miss Haynes will be with you in a moment,' her maid announced, coming through from the bedroom. 'She is with her dressmaker at present.'

Davidson nodded, and took up the newspaper mechanically from the table. The room seemed to him almost faint with the perfume of flowers. He glanced around carelessly, and suddenly found his attention riveted upon her writing-table. In a little silver vase, standing by itself, was the red rose which he had bought for her two days since!

Chapter 37

She came to him in a few moments, dressed in a fascinating negligée gown, - came to him with a rustle of silk and a faint expression of surprise upon her upraised eyebrows.

'I didn't expect you until this evening,' she said.

'I took the liberty of coming here to ask you a question.'

She smiled as she sat down upon the sofa. 'Oh, the paper is quite safe.'

'How did you know what I came for?' he said, a little startled.

'My dear friend,' she said, shrugging her shoulders, 'as I have decided that it is to my interests to link my future with yours, you cannot wonder that I have found such details as those' - she pointed to an evening paper which he noticed now lying upon her writing-table - 'interesting. I have been trying to understand how matters stand. Tell me if I'm right! It seems to me that so long as that document remains an imagined thing, so long as it is not produced or sworn to definitely, you are safe.'

'The corporation is safe,' Davidson said, 'and in a way, I suppose, I am. On the other hand, I'll be accused, naturally, of suppressing it, and probably of complicity in Austin's murder. There is van Heerden, you see, prepared to swear that Austin came to London with that paper in his possession.

Austin is known to have come to my office. He has certainly been murdered. The paper cannot be found, and the corporation remains in possession of the mine. People will certainly put these things together.'

She nodded. 'It will be very bad indeed,' she said slowly, 'for your reputation.'

'It will, I'm afraid,' Davidson said, 'considerably lessen my social value as your husband.'

'It seems to me,' she replied, 'that money is so powerful. I dare say you will be able to live it down.'

'With your help,' Davidson said sarcastically, 'it seems to me very possible. By the bye,' he continued, 'with reference to that document, you must forgive me if I feel some slight uneasiness at times as to its safety.'

'You need have none,' she said. 'It is in safe keeping.'

'It is your own interests as well as mine you are guarding,' he reminded her.

'I'm perfectly aware of it,' she said. 'Since you are here, may I offer you some tea?'

'Thanks,' he said, 'I think not. By the bye, do you care to go to the Opera to-night? I have two stalls.'

A sudden light flashed over her face. It was as though the mask had been raised for a moment. Perhaps by contrast her tone seemed colder than ever as she said him. 'I'd like to very much. Will you call for me?'

'At half-past seven,' he said. 'We will have a little dinner somewhere first.'

'You are sure,' she said, 'that you do not mind being seen out?'

'It is all to my advantage,' he said. 'The men who are most talked about should never shrink from publicity. The people who have been told today that I'm a bankrupt, a swindler, and a murderer, and that my ruin is only a matter of minutes, will hesitate if they see me with you in the stalls of the Opera to-night.'

'Nero fiddled,' she reminded him.

'Nero was a hysterical person,' he said. 'My tendencies are towards the other extreme. Until half-past seven, then.'

'Until half-past seven,' she repeated.

He bowed and left her without even shaking hands. She stood quite still for a moment, looking at the door which he had closed behind him. Then she crossed the room slowly, and lifted the vase with its solitary rose to her lips. A second later it lay dashed to pieces upon the floor, the flaming colour was in her cheeks, her fists were clenched.

'I hate him!' she said to herself. 'I hate him now more than ever!'

Eileen talked more than usual at the short dinner which they had at a restaurant close to the Opera House. Davidson, a little weary with the strain of the day, was at first unresponsive, but gradually he forgot himself in the interest of playing his new part. She was wearing a dress of black velvet, a rope of pearls which had been sent for her inspection only that afternoon, and pearl earrings, concerning which she gravely said his opinion. There was something a little exotic about her to-night, - about the small, delicate head with the masses of brown hair, the pale complexion, the deep eyes with their hidden depths, the pearls which fell gracefully

241

over her black gown. Many people knew him by sight, and pointed him out to others, - the man whom everyone was talking about, the man who was supposed to be shivering on the brink of social and financial ruin, whose very freedom from justice might be a matter of hours, - sitting there with a girl who was unknown to all of them, yet without a doubt one of his own world! Some of them wondered that she should care to be seen about with him at such a time. These, however, were mostly the men. The women, who saw him as usual, well-groomed, good-looking, debonair, only admired him the more for his courage.

They had driven the few yards together to the Opera House in silence. Nevertheless, Davidson fancied that his companion seemed to-night a little more accessible. He was amazed to find how great an interest he was beginning to take in her moods, amazed to find himself taking every opportunity to touch her fingers, to speak covertly of the destined ending of their engagement. He fancied sometimes that her fingers rested more softly in his, that the chill aloofness of her demeanour had been more than once on the point of being raised. And yet, after all, it might only be fancy, he thought, as he followed her and the attendant along the corridor into their places. He was a fool to trouble himself about it. She was very likely what she had always seemed, - a bloodless, indifferent creature, with a greed for jewels and fine clothes sprung up in her, - a fungus growth, the evil result of her long years of servitude. Yet that night his convictions as to her coldness received something of a shock. It was the first night they had been to the Opera together, and he had imagined that she would sit as she had sat through so many theatres, - slightly bored, slightly nonchalant, interested only to know who the people might be by whom they were surrounded, and in the play itself if by chance it was well acted and satisfactory. To-night, he realized that there were things which could move her, even if he himself had not the power. He saw her eyes flash with the glory of the music, and he saw them turn marvellously soft and tender as the white-robed Iseult sang to them with sobs in her throat, sobs which seemed to make that melody only more intense and sweeter. She seemed to respond to every note of the music. More than once he saw her quiver with excitement. By accident her fingers touched his and rested there. He felt a thrill which amazed him. For the moment he, too, forgot that wretched maze of affairs in which he was plunged. The great passionate love-story throbbed, too, in his heart and veins. The figures on the stage were for a moment dim. They existed only as types. In those few seconds he realized, for the first time in his life, the real meaning of this wonderful emotion with which the very air around them seemed charged, and almost at the moment of realization there came to him fiercely, insistently, the great question, - did she share it, did she understand, was it possible that such a passion could be born of itself, without response or encouragement? He leaned forward, and tried to see into her face. A great stillness reigned in the half-darkened Opera House, a stillness except for the wonderful music which still flowed from those divine lips. He leaned forward until he could see her face, and his heart throbbed with the wonder of it! All the passion, all the intense mystery of a strenuous love were there in her glowing eyes, her half-parted lips! It was only a momentary glimpse he had. Then, as though conscious of his observation, she raised her fan. Their eyes had never met. He was left, after all, with the problem unsolved!

Davidson came down to earth again as the curtain fell. His companion drew a long, soft breath, and leaned back in her seat.

'Don't you want to go out and smoke or something?' she said calmly. 'I do not feel like talking at all. The music is wonderful!'

He left her without a word. Only as he reached the end of his row and turned to walk up the sloping aisle, he glanced back once more. She had not moved. Her eyes were closed. She seemed, indeed, like a person exhausted with the strain of listening. He made his way out to the refreshment room, humming softly to himself. It was a mask, after all, which she wore! He understood suddenly the relief which had come to him. He understood that this engagement, which had seemed to him like a piece of half-contemptible bathos, had suddenly become the first and most desirable thing in his life!

Chapter 38

The lawyer sat in a comfortable easy-chair adjoining Davidson's writing-table. His manner was serious, but not discouraging.

'You see, Davidson,' he said, 'after all, it depends very much upon this alleged document. The whole case practically hinges upon it. If the defendants are unable to procure it, or a copy of it, or witnesses who can swear to it, I do not think that they can do us much harm, especially if we take the course which I have already suggested to our counsel. As yet we have received no intimation that the other side have the slightest trace of the document in question. If, on the other hand, it should come into their possession, they are bound to notify us. May I ask, Mr. Davidson, what you believe the probabilities are as regards this matter?'

'It isn't a matter of probability,' Davidson said. 'To the best of my belief, there is no such document in existence.'

'In that case,' the lawyer continued, 'I think that you need have no further anxiety about the case. Of course, there is no chance of a long sentence for the defendant. You understand that?'

'Perfectly,' Davidson said. 'I don't wish it. I'd not have prosecuted him at all, but it seemed the only way to stop what might have grown into a serious annoyance.'

'I'm sorry,' the lawyer said, 'that the whole thing seems to have been taken so seriously by the Press and the public. I see your shares have dropped to a ridiculous amount.'

'A chance for someone to make money,' Davidson said. 'I'm much obliged to you for coming up, Shackleton.'

The lawyer nodded and took his departure. Davidson sat for some time in a brown study. Fundamentally he had all the direct impulses and propensities of a truthful man. The course of action into which he was at present driven was distasteful - almost repugnant to him. Yet, after all, he was only fighting van Heerden with his own weapons. The man was a blackmailer, - nothing more or less. Yet the fact did not seem to Davidson to make his hands the cleaner. And there was the girl! The memory of her face haunted him, her desperate plight had been only too apparent. If that document of Austin's was worth the paper it was written on, it was he who was the supplanter, the thief, morally responsible for her grievous plight! He moved in his chair uneasily. It was almost a relief when the phone rang.

'Is that Mr. Davidson?' a woman's voice said.

'Yes!' he said.

'Mr. Malcolm Davidson?'

'Yes, - what is it?' he said quickly.

There was a moment's silence. The terrified voice, which had still seemed somehow familiar to him, was silent. He could hear from the room to which the instrument was connected, the musical chiming of a Swiss clock - the call of a bird - and then silence. His hand was upon the receiver to ring up the Exchange when suddenly a cry of terror, a cry of shrill, agonized terror, rang in his ear.

'Malcolm! Mr. Davidson! Malcolm! Come -'

There was an abrupt cessation of that frantic cry. The last word was muffled, as though something had been dashed against the speaker's mouth. There was the sound of the falling of a chair or heavy piece of furniture. Then silence! - silence ominous, heavy, maddening!

Davidson rang up the Exchange. The young lady who said him was a little annoyed at his vehemence.

'I want you to tell me to whom I have been speaking!' he said 'Where was I rung up from a few moments ago?'

'No idea,' the young lady said tartly. 'Didn't they give their name?'

'I want to know where the call was from,' Davidson said. 'Please tell me quickly.'

'We don't take any note of local calls,' the young lady said. 'Ring off, please!'

'Stop!' Davidson cried. 'Listen, please! This is important! I'm Mr. Davidson - Mr. Malcolm Davidson - of the Incorporated Mines Association. I have just been rung up by a woman in distress - someone who appealed for help. She was dragged away from the phone before she could tell me where she was speaking from. You must try and find out the number for me. You must do it! It may be a matter of life or death!'

There was an instant's silence - a buzzing noise - then a man's voice. 'Sorry, sir,' he said, 'our operator cannot remember the exact number that was speaking to you. It was a house in Farringford Square, though. She's sure of that.'

Davidson left the office in such a hurry that a whole crop of fresh rumours were started. He drove as swiftly as his electric taxi could take him to the corner of Farringford Square. All the time with a phone directory on his knee, he was copying out addresses. He entered Farringford Square on foot, with the paper in his hand. There were twenty-eight addresses. He had no idea where to begin.

Seven or eight were the addresses of business firms. He struck these out. Then he tried the others. One after the other he interviewed all sorts of people unsuccessfully. He was received everywhere with suspicion. Most of the houses were converted flats or cheap lodging-houses. Half-dressed women leered at him over the banisters; shabby men of all ages were slavishly anxious to earn a tip. Gradually he was forced to realize that his was a mad, almost hopeless search. People stood at their doors and watched him, jeering. Women hung out of the windows, shouting coarse invitations or derisive comments upon his perseverance. His nerves were all on edge, his blood was hot with anger. Somewhere within a few hundred, perhaps a few yards of him, this girl was in the hands of persons who meant ill to her. The terror in her voice was no ordinary fear. She was face to face with the worst that could happen.

He reached the last house on his list. It was on the further side of the square, and one of the most respectable in appearance. Contrary to what was apparently the usual custom, the front door was closed, and most of the blinds drawn. There was no sign of life about the place when he rang the bell. Yet after scarcely a moment's delay the door was thrown open, and a neatly dressed parlour maid said his summons.

Davidson adopted new tactics. He drew a sovereign from his waistcoat pocket, and held it between his fingers. 'You are on the phone, of course. Someone rang me up from here about an hour or so ago. I recognized the voice, but the message was indistinct. Will you tell Miss Haynes that I'm here?'

The girl shook her head. 'There is no one of that name living here, sir,' she said.

'A rather pale young lady, tall and slim, who has just arrived,' Davidson persisted. 'I'm anxious to find her quickly. Can't you help me?'

He pulled out a handful of gold, and the girl looked at it with covetous eyes. She sighed as she once more shook her head.

'There is no one here of that name, sir,' she said, - 'no young lady at all, in fact.'

'You are quite sure?' Davidson said, with a sinking heart.

'Quite, sir,' the girl said confidently.

She made a movement as though to close the door. It is possible that Davidson would have taken the hint and departed, but for that last searching look which he threw at her. He thrust his boot against the door, and resumed his place on the inner side of the threshold. From there he looked at her once more. He was right. There were traces of powder on her cheeks, and her eyebrows were certainly not natural.

'I'd like to see your mistress before I go,' Davidson said firmly. 'Please go and tell her. I'll not keep her more than a few moments.'

'She's not in,' the girl said, with a distinct change of manner. 'Please don't stay about here or I'll get into trouble.'

'I'm sorry,' Davidson said, 'but if she is not in, I'm going to wait for her.'

He was in the hall now, - a miserable, untidy place with a broken-down mirror and hat-rack as sole furniture, and covered with a much soiled oilcloth. The stairs were right ahead of him, and Davidson looked up. He looked into a woman's face as she leaned over the well of the banisters, looking down. Almost immediately she drew away and came down.

Davidson rose up to meet her. She was dressed in black, was very pale, with large earrings, - pretty in a way, and certainly not of formidable appearance.

'You wished to see me?' she said, a little hesitatingly, as she reached the bottom stair. 'I thought I heard you say you wished to speak to her mistress.'

'You are right, madam,' Davidson said. 'I do wish to speak to you.'

'And what is it that you wish?' the lady said.

'An act of kindness,' Davidson said, 'for which I'm willing to pay - to pay heavily. I'm in search of a young lady who rang me up only an hour or so ago from this locality, - I believe from this house. I'm offering a reward of two hundred pounds for anyone who may help me in my search.'

He raised his voice. He meant the servant, or the person who was posing as a servant, to hear him. He was unable to observe her closely, but he noticed that she moved a little nearer, and appeared to be listening intently.

'I'm afraid that you have come to the wrong house,' the lady said gently. 'This is not a very nice neighbourhood, I know, but we are quite respectable people here, and we are not upon the phone at all.'

'Not on the phone at all?' Davidson repeated. 'But I have your name and number from the phone directory, Mrs. Garside!'

'Mrs. Garside has left,' the woman said. 'I have taken the house, but the phone was of no use to me, so I have had it taken away.'

'May I see the place where the instrument was?' Davidson said. 'I have a particular reason for asking.'

'Certainly not!' the lady said, a little sharply. 'Open the door, Hilda. We have nothing else to say to you, sir.'

The maid obeyed, and Davidson reluctantly took up his hat. He was already upon the threshold when he suddenly stopped. A remarkable change came over him. He stepped quickly back. The woman had gone as pale as death. From one of the rooms upstairs came the shrill, unmistakable summons of a phone and mingling with it the chiming of a cuckoo clock.

'Shut the door,' Davidson ordered sternly. 'Madam,' he said, turning towards the lady of the house, 'it is still within your power to earn that two hundred pounds!'

The woman looked at him curiously. 'Two hundred pounds,' she said, 'is a great deal of money. One does not carry about sums like that.'

Davidson thrust his hand into his pocket, and drew out a little roll of notes. 'I have twelve ten-pound notes here,' he said, 'and I can write a cheque for the balance. You know what I want. If you turn me away, I'll be back with a search warrant in less than half-an-hour.'

She held out her hand for the notes. 'Follow me,' she said. 'You understand that I'm simply a lodging-house keeper. I cannot be responsible for my tenants or their actions.'

'I understand that,' Davidson said eagerly. 'Quick! Lead the way upstairs.'

Chapter 39

Davidson followed his guide up two flights of stairs, - on the landing of the third she paused.

'I don't usually interfere with the comings and goings of my lodgers,' she said. 'They pay for their rooms. That is all I ask. You see the door opposite you?'

'Yes!' Davidson said quickly.

'That room is tenanted by a young woman who called herself Montague, but received letters under the name of Austin. She had a visitor this afternoon who might be the young person of whom you are in search. You had better go in and see.'

Davidson was across the landing in a moment. He tapped sharply upon the door. There was no answer. He tried the handle. The door was locked!

'Open the door,' he cried out, shaking it vigorously.

There was no answer. To Davidson the silence was ominous. He turned to the woman who stood silently by his side, with a fierce little exclamation. 'Where is the phone?' he said.

'Inside there,' she said. 'It used to be my sitting-room.'

'The door is locked!' he said

'I do not understand it,' she admitted.

'Have you another key?'

'No!'

He flung himself at the door, tearing it half from its hinges. Another assault, and with a tearing of splinters it fell inside. Davidson stepped over it into the room, and a low cry of anger broke from his lips. The woman at his side fled shrieking downstairs. On the floor lay Eileen Haynes, her limbs bound with cords, a gag in her mouth, her clothing all dishevelled, her eyes shining with an almost painful intensity from her ashen grey face. Davidson fell on his knees by her side.

'Eileen!' he said 'My God!'

He snatched his knife from his pocket, removed the gag from her mouth, and cut all her bonds. Her hands tried nervously to rearrange her dress over her bosom. He tore off his own coat and threw it over her.

'Are you badly hurt?' he said anxiously.

'I'm not hurt much,' she said weakly, 'but -'

'But what?' he said.

She started to cry softly but insistently. Black fear rose up to torture him. 'But what?' he repeated, with sinking heart.

'It has gone!' she said, crossing her hands upon her bosom.

'What has gone?' he said. 'Quick!'

'The deed!' she whispered. 'Don't look at me like that. I couldn't help it. It was a trap, of course, to get me here, and I was a fool. The letter was from you, but I ought to have known that it was a forgery. I was taken unawares. She was like a madwoman. She would have torn the clothes from my body. I struggled. I called out. It was no use. She has taken it away.'

'But you are not hurt?' he exclaimed anxiously.

'I - no!' she said, a little vacantly. 'But it is gone! I was not fit to be trusted with it. I ought to have given it up to you.'

She was very pale, and he was afraid of her fainting. He summoned the landlady once more. She was waiting on the stairs close by.

'Something very serious has happened here,' he said, sternly. 'This young lady has been assaulted and robbed.'

'I'm sure I'm very sorry,' the woman said. 'You can't blame any of us, though. I never heard a sound, no more did Hilda, and I can't prevent my lodgers having visitors.'

'We won't discuss it,' Davidson said sharply. 'But if this is Miss Montague's room, -'

'It isn't,' the woman interrupted. 'It's my sitting-room. Miss Montague has only an attic, and she came to me and said that she couldn't receive a visitor there, and said me to lend her my room for a few minutes.'

Davidson nodded. 'The other rooms on this floor are unoccupied, of course,' he said. 'Oh! It's quite easy to understand. I don't need to ask you any more questions. I don't want any more explanations. If you want to keep this out of the police court, you will do exactly as I tell you.'

'Yes!' she exclaimed eagerly. 'I will do anything.'

'Send for a taxi cab,' Davidson said, 'and arrange this young lady's dress so that I can take her home.'

Eileen had risen to her feet, and was sitting in an easy-chair. She was leaning forward, with her face half buried in her hands. Davidson turned towards her.

'Eileen -'

She avoided his gaze. 'Don't!' she begged. 'Please don't talk to me. I can't bear it.'

'But I may say - ' he began.

'No!' she interrupted, almost fiercely. 'Please say nothing. I mean it. I cannot bear to talk! I cannot bear to be talked to!'

A little throb of anger darkened his face. She had not even common gratitude for her rescue! She had but one thought, one regret, - the loss of that future of luxury to attain which she had bound herself to him. A curious anger burned in his blood, - a pain which he could not analyse shook his heart. Then there came the sound of voices on the stairs, feminine voices raised in anger! The door was burst open. Hannah stood there upon the threshold, looking in upon them, her lips curved in an ugly smile of triumph, her eyes ablaze. Behind her stood the landlady, a black bodice in her hand, her forehead wrinkled in a deprecating frown.

'So you've found her, have you?' Hannah exclaimed, her face turned towards Davidson, her finger outstretched to where Eileen sat shrinking back in her chair. 'Thieves, both of you! Thieves! Thieves!'

Davidson pointed to Eileen's torn clothing. 'And that?' he said.

'It was restitution,' the girl said fiercely. 'The deed was mine! Your millions are mine! She stole it for you - her brother was a murderer for you! How do you think the story will look in the newspapers, eh? Inciting to murder and theft! Isn't that a crime? Swindlers, both of you!' she cried passionately. 'You'd have kept me a beggar, eh,' she cried to Eileen, 'while you clad your poor body in silks and laces, covered yourself with jewels and made him marry you? And I was to starve! - to starve or worse! Well, we'll see! We'll see!'

'Young lady,' Davidson said calmly, 'you are being led away by your imagination. You have taken a paper away from Miss Haynes which you seem to think is going to turn out a sort of El Dorado. It isn't worth the paper it's written on.'

'It's a lie!' the girl shrieked. 'I've taken it to the lawyers. It is genuine - they all say so.'

Davidson almost lifted Eileen from her chair. 'That remains to be seen,' he said.

'In any case, it was stolen!' she cried. 'That young woman there has got to say how it came into her possession, and what she meant by going around with it sewn into her bodice! Oh, you needn't try to dupe me!' she cried. 'I want my money - God knows how I want it! And I mean to make her suffer, too!' she added, pointing to Eileen. 'She's a thief! She's lived in luxury while I've starved; - she's worn the clothes of a princess while I've gone in rags! But she shall pay! My God, she shall pay!'

Davidson, with Eileen by his side, had reached the door. 'I'm afraid,' he said turning to the girl, who was still regarding them with breathless anger, 'that you have let your imagination run away with you a good deal. A dose of the law courts will do you no harm. If you care for a word of warning from me, you can have it: don't build your hopes too much upon that paper!'

'We shall see!' she cried fiercely. 'You can't frighten me! If the paper is of no value, why did she steal it, why did she carry it sewn in her clothes? If you -'

She hesitated for a moment. Her eyes rested upon Davidson, her expression softened. 'If you want to make terms - ' she began.

He turned away. 'Come, Eileen,' he said.

In the cab they scarcely spoke. She had the air of a person utterly exhausted, - indifferent to anything that might happen.

'Tell me,' he said, soon after they started, 'what made you go to that house?'

'The letter from you,' she said. 'I was a fool, of course, but I went. It doesn't matter, does it?'

'I suppose not,' he said.

The despair in her face nerved him to further speech. 'I'm afraid,' he said, 'that you are worrying about that deed - or rather the loss of it. I'm sorry that I came too late, but it couldn't be helped. You did all that you could! I'm sure of that.'

'Of course!' she interposed impatiently. 'And I have failed! That's the end of it!'

He looked out of the window. The sun had ceased to shine. He seemed suddenly to realize the reason for her dejection. She believed that he was indeed a pauper. It was for the wreck of her hopes that she was lamenting. The rest went for nothing. He was a poor man - no longer of any interest to her! His manner unconsciously stiffened as the thought came rushing home to him. He drew away from her, and he remained silent until the cab stopped in front of her

258

hotel. She stepped out quickly, and almost ran across the pavement.

'Tomorrow,' she said, holding out her hand as though to prevent his following.

He bowed and turned away. Already he was beginning to find excuses for her. Nevertheless, he watched the slim, swaying figure, as the doors closed upon her, with something of apprehension. Was it ominous that she should pass away without a backward glance? Was she indeed nothing but an adventuress, deprived of her prey?

He paid the cab and walked slowly back to his rooms. His solicitor had already rung up. Two of his directors were waiting to see him, a reporter buttonholed him on the pavement. From all of which Davidson knew that Hannah Austin had lost no time, that the first note of battle had been sounded!

Chapter 40

Miss Haynes had left two hours ago, and had taken all her luggage and paid her bill. Apparently she had no idea of returning - at any rate, she had not reserved any rooms. The hall-porter of the little hotel looked at Davidson with some curiosity as he said his rapid questions. The manageress came rustling out of her office and beamed on Davidson, who had once stayed there for several weeks. She confirmed the information which he had already received, and supplemented it with a few further details.

'Miss Haynes paid her bill?' Davidson said.

'Certainly, sir,' the manageress said. 'Miss Haynes was exceedingly particular about paying her accounts the moment they were presented.'

'And she left no message?' Davidson said.

'None at all, sir,' was the answer.

He noticed the gleam of curiosity in her eyes, and promptly altered his tactics. 'Thank you very much,' he said, turning away. 'I quite understood that Miss Haynes was not leaving until this afternoon. My mistake, I dare say. By the bye, have you any instructions with regard to letters?'

'None,' the manageress replied. 'If any come, we shall keep them until we hear from her.'

Davidson turned away and re-entered his taxi. 'I'll find a note at my rooms, I dare say,' he said. 'Good morning.'

His words were prophetic. He called at his rooms on his way to the club for lunch, and found a note there addressed to him in Eileen's handwriting:

Wednesday morning.

You will understand, of course, that this is the end. The jewels which you gave me I have said today by registered post. One ring I have kept. It is, I think, the least valuable of any, but I did not wish to part with it. If you insist, however, it is always at your disposal.

I'm going back where I belong - to the world which I'd never have quitted. Everything has been a great mistake. Please understand that you are absolutely and entirely free in every way. I only trust that I may live long enough to atone in some measure for my folly.

Eileen Haynes.

Davidson read this letter over a dozen times. One thing alone seemed clear. She had deserted him. She had not even waited for the final issue. She had fled from the sinking ship with a haste almost indecent. She had made no terms, suggested no compromise. Davidson, when he thought the whole matter over, was still puzzled. Such haste was not logical. If his hand was no longer strong enough to open the gates of the Promised Land, it could at least have lifted her up from the miseries of her past life. He found himself, after a study of her few lines, curiously depressed. She had gone - willingly - apparently without regret except for her wasted opportunities. He felt an emptiness in his life which he failed to understand. There had been nothing of the sort when Lady Catherine had held out her hand and bidden him farewell. Was he getting sentimental? He set his teeth. Absurd! It was an episode happily concluded! Outside there was thunder in the air - a storm for him to face!

His solicitor did not beat about the bush. 'In the face of that document, Mr. Davidson,' he said, 'the Treasury do not propose to proceed with the prosecution of van Heerden. Its existence, of course, throws altogether a different light upon the whole situation, whatever may be its exact legal worth. Van Heerden was simply engaged upon a task of compromise. He had something solid behind him. There is not a shadow of evidence against him.'

'Very well,' Davidson said, 'let van Heerden go. I admit that when I sent to Scotland Yard I never anticipated that this particular document would ever come into evidence.'

'You knew of its existence?' the lawyer said.

'Austin himself showed it to me,' Davidson said calmly. 'So far as Austin himself was concerned the affair was a swindle, for it was he who recommended me to jump the claim - said he thought that there was some stuff there, but he had no money to work it. I let him off a hundred pounds he owed me, and took his advice. But that is ancient history. The mine is my property - or it was.'

Shackleton listened with a grave face. 'Davidson,' he said, 'I hope and believe that you are speaking the truth, but the original deed is in the hands of unscrupulous people. We had a notification this afternoon that a suit is about to be started against your corporation.'

'The sooner the better,' Davidson said. 'We'll know where we are, at any rate. My claim clear. By the statute laws of the country that claim was forfeit. If it wasn't, then inducing me to sink capital into the business and work the claim was a conspiracy.'

'Your corporation fights with you, of course?' the lawyer said.

'Of course,' Davidson said. 'What else could they do? We fight to the end!'

That night, shares in the Incorporated Mines Association stood at 90. At closing time the following day they stood at 74. A few lines in the paper had done it. An action had been started by van Heerden, and the legatees of the estate of the late Richard Austin, claiming as their property the Letlakana Mine. The thing had been talked about for some time, but now that it had actually occurred, people seemed none the less staggered. The city believed in Malcolm Davidson - it had believed in him so implicitly that in its heart it had never placed any faith in the rumours. Yet there it was now in black and white. It was no longer possible to speak of compromise. The matter was to be fought out in the open courts, and failure could spell nothing but ruin to one of the richest corporations in London. Davidson's photograph was in all the papers - also the menu of a famous dinner which he gave to his directors. He sent a cheque for five thousand pounds to a hospital, and was reported to be going on the turf. The lawsuit he treated everywhere as a joke. He was careful always to wear the usual bunch of violets in his buttonhole, and to affect something of the dandy in his attire. His personal demeanour kept his shares at least ten points higher than they would otherwise have been.

But Davidson, nevertheless, was in hell! He was badgered by his directors, worried by his lawyers, and underneath it all, and apart from his financial responsibilities, he was suffering from a sense of personal loss, a wound whose pain left him but little peace. He never stopped to admit to himself exactly what his suffering was. He sat for hours lost in thought, and his thoughts were always of that pale lady of his dreams who had stolen so abruptly from his arms, the girl who had played for a few weeks so strange a part in his life. He tried to find what had become of her, but in vain; she seemed to have completely vanished. He puzzled over her behaviour until the lines in his face grew set and hard. Was she indeed ingrate - ready to abandon her strange bargain at the first whisper of disaster? Or had she some other reason? He had accepted her terms because of the power which she held - what if, at the loss of that power, she had taken it for granted that their bargain was cancelled, and had hurried away to avoid the shame of dismissal from him! It was just what she would do - perhaps just what she had done!

Davidson was careful, during these days of probation, to attend at his office regularly, and to shrink from none of his customary duties. One afternoon his clerk brought him in a card.

'A young lady to see you, sir!' he announced.

Davidson's heart gave a jump, the blood rushed through his veins, and he was scarcely able to read the card which he had taken into his fingers with well-affected carelessness. Then the pain came, the black disappointment which seemed to turn his heart into a stone. It was not she! He found it hard to take any interest in this caller, and yet he felt that her coming was significant.

Miss Hannah Austin.

'You can show the young lady in,' Davidson ordered.

When she arrived, Davidson scarcely knew her. She was expensively dressed from head to foot. She carried herself with an assurance which was almost overdone. The fashion of her dress and hat were certainly not chosen with a view to being overlooked. She was very modern - she reminded him exactly of a young lady in a musical comedy with whom he had once had a slight acquaintance. He would scarcely have been surprised had he found, when she lifted her veil, that her eyebrows were blackened.

'You didn't expect to see me, of course,' she said, holding his hand for a moment, and looking at him steadfastly. 'May I sit down?'

'Of course,' he said.

She chose the easy-chair, and crossed her legs with a good deal of rustle and a considerable display of black silk stocking.

She looked at him curiously. 'Are you still angry with me?' she said.

'Well, I don't usually bear malice,' he said, 'but I can scarcely forgive your method of dealing with Miss Haynes!'

'Or its results?' she said, with a little laugh. 'Well, I came out on the top, anyhow, and you must remember, Mr.

Davidson, that I was desperate, - you don't know how desperate,' she continued, after a moment's pause. 'I hadn't a penny left in the world! - not apenny! - not a friend! And somewhere in London there was wealth that belonged to me!'

'That,' Davidson said dryly, 'is a matter which is as yet undecided.'

'Well, I judge by facts,' she said with a little laugh. 'Lawyers don't usually throw money away, do they? They're willing to advance me all I want on the security of the Letlakana Mine.'

Davidson smiled upon her genially. 'My mine,' he said.

'No!' she said, 'the property of the legatees of Richard Austin!'

Davidson shook his head. 'My dear young lady,' he said, 'you were more in your element when you walked bareheaded upon the sands, and saved me from a soaking.'

'And you,' she said, 'were nicer to me, a great deal, for those few days.'

'Naturally,' he said, smiling. 'How can I be particularly amiable to a young lady who is trying to ruin me?'

She looked at him earnestly. In her fashionable attire she presented a very different appearance from the eager, brown-skinned girl, with the shapely limbs whom he had first seen. Yet he fancied that she was trying to reawaken his earlier impressions of her, - innocent of vanity as he was, he could not misunderstand her appealing gaze!

'I don't want to ruin you,' she said. 'Isn't there enough for both of us? Why should we fight?'

He sighed. 'How can we compromise?' he said. 'The mine doesn't belong to me any longer. I sold it years ago to the Incorporated Mines Association.'

'You could not sell what didn't belong to you,' she objected.

'They paid me the money for it, at any rate,' he said.

'If I win,' she said, 'who will lose the money?'

'The Incorporated Mines Association,' he said, 'but they would have a claim upon me. I suppose, eventually, that I'd.'

She held out her hand - no longer brown and stained with seaweed, but delicately gloved, perfumed, elegant. 'Let's be friends,' she said. 'I'm sorry I was rough to your little ally! I couldn't help it. She was in my way. I chose the only means. We needn't consider her, - you and I are different sort of people. We know what we want. I'm not only a money grubber. I want the rest of life, the whole thing, - the music, the passion! Remember my wretched, starved existence! Do you wonder that I'm on fire to pass on to the other things? It isn't the money - your money or anyone else's! I want life! Can't you understand? You must! - you must!'

Her passionate eyes sought his, her body swayed towards him. Davidson looked downwards at his blotter. In the outer office he could hear the clicking of typewriters, the subdued murmur of voices. Through the half-opened window came floating in the daily chorus, - footsteps upon the pavement, the ringing of bicycle bells, the far-off roar of the heavier traffic. All these things seemed to him curiously unreal. He was conscious only of the intensity of the moment, the pleading of her eyes, the warm breath upon his cheeks.

He heard the rustling of her skirts. He felt that she was rising from her chair. Then he braced himself for his effort.

'My dear young lady,' he said, - 'if you really want to compromise - for a moderate amount - I will send for my lawyer. We can't arrange this thing by ourselves.'

She rose to her feet, and was speechless. When he looked at her face, he found it almost unrecognisable. The flash of her eyes was in itself a threat.

'I'm sorry,' he said lamely. 'I hope you understand.'

She turned to the door, and went out without a word.

Chapter 41

Davidson stood at last on the other side of those long, dragging months of unspeakable weariness. Day after day, in the close atmosphere of the Courts, week after week of what seemed to him unnecessary repetitions and delays, - so the great machine of the law moved on its slow and stately way, and the case of Austin v. The Incorporated Mines Association crept on toward the end. One thing at least Davidson had gained. His examination and cross-examination - and he was in the witness box altogether for nearly two days - failed to reveal a single weak joint in the armour of his truthfulness. His story was consistent and honourable throughout. He was able to prove the payment to Austin, to prove Austin's suggestion that he should have a try at the mine. At the end of the case, one thing remained certain, and that was that morally speaking the mine was Davidson's when he had sold it to the Corporation. Yet behind it all there were those title-deeds, with which Austin had never parted, and which now formed the backbone of this present suit. The more sensational part of the case, too, concerning which there had been endless rumours, collapsed immediately.

'Isn't it true that Austin paid you a visit at your offices a few days before his murder?' counsel said.

'Certainly!' Davidson said.

'Will you tell us what transpired at that interview?'

'Well, it scarcely amounted to an interview,' Davidson said composedly. 'The man was drunk, and I found him offensive. He brandished the document at me on which the present case is founded, and I suspected him of an attempt at blackmail. I had him thrown out.'

'Yet a few days afterwards you commissioned Haynes - the man who murdered Austin - to obtain that document from him,' counsel said,

There was chatter in the courtroom.

'Scarcely that,' Davidson said. 'Haynes, who had been a friend of mine in South Africa, and was a man of an altogether different stamp than Austin, called upon me a few days later. I told him the circumstances.'

'You incited him to procure that document from Austin,' counsel said.

'Not so,' Davidson said. 'I told him that I had declined to be blackmailed by Austin, but that after all I would prefer to pay a reasonable sum of money for the document in question. Haynes had been on more friendly terms with Austin than any of us, and I thought that he might induce him to listen to reason.'

'If the document was valueless, why should you bother about it?'

'I'm afraid that you don't know much about the mining world,' Davidson replied amiably. 'Any prejudicial report, however malicious, however false, affects the market, and one must always consider one's stockholders.'

'Very well, then,' counsel said, 'we come to this. You deputed Haynes to see what he could do with Austin. Do you realize your responsibility in this matter? You are aware of what happened?'

'Certainly,' Davidson said. 'I'll never cease to regret it. Austin was mad drunk and the two men quarrelled. The blow which killed him was struck in self-defence.'

'The law did not take that view.'

'I stood by Haynes when he died,' Davidson said. 'He told me the truth then, and the truth is what I have told you.'

'Nevertheless, he stole the document,' counsel continued. 'It was discovered afterwards in the possession of Miss Haynes.'

'So I have heard,' Davidson said calmly. 'It was a pity that she didn't hand it over to me.'

'You would have destroyed it, I suppose?'

'For sure!' Davidson said. 'The mine belonged to me. Austin had said before witnesses that there were no papers, that the claim had not been worked for the requisite time; and, therefore, by the mining laws of the country my purchase was good.'

The case lasted well over the Christmas recess.

During the holidays, Davidson spent a good part of his time seeking for some trace of Eileen Haynes. He went himself to her old employers, but they were able to tell him nothing. They could only show him the testimonial which they had written at her request, and which she had taken away with her a few days after her departure from the hotel. There was no one who seemed able to help him. Regretfully, he called in the services of a private detective, who, however, was equally unsuccessful. The holidays passed, the case was reopened, and Davidson was once more immersed in the struggle.

Then it was over at last. The strain remained, - the judge declined to pronounce judgement immediately. It might be three days or it might be even more than two weeks before his decision was reached.

Davidson turned away from the court with a strong desire for solitude. The suspense long drawn out through the weeks and through the months, had become unbearable. He felt himself no longer able calmly to discuss the pros and the cons of the case with his fellow directors and friends. He was sick to death of it all. He escaped from one or two passers-by, and a reporter or so who tried to buttonhole him, and jumped into a taxi. A few brief orders, a pencilled note to Carter, and Davidson, leaving the garage by the other entrance, took the Underground to its terminus, walked out into the country, and was caught up within an hour by the car, in which Carter was sitting on the front seat by the side of the chauffeur.

The evening passed swiftly into night as they drove fast up the motorway. Davidson leaned back in his seat, with both windows down, feeling an inexpressible relief in the sharp sting of the night air. He was free at last from the hateful stifling environment of the last few months. No longer was there anyone to point him out as the man who had sold for several million pounds a mine which had never belonged to him. Save for the two motionless figures in front, he was alone. There was no one to ask him wearisome questions, no one to offer him sympathy or wish him good-fortune. Davidson ordered the driver to exit the motorway

On they sped through the night, till the villages were like dead haunts, without a light in the windows, and only an occasional lamp-post to mark the place where men slumbered. They passed through a town, which was like a city of the dead, and on again to the wilder country, where the rabbits rushed, terrified, before the streaming lights of the car, and the wind alone, of all Nature's voices, seemed left to remind him that this was not a world of ghosts through which he rushed.

Presently he saw the man at the wheel swerve a little in his seat, and he lifted the speaking-tube to his lips. 'Can we get through, Murray,' he said, 'or shall we stop?'

'We can get through, sir,' the man replied, 'if we can rest for half-an-hour somewhere.'

They went to a hotel, and the two men ordered food and drink. Davidson himself drank a long whisky and soda. Then they rushed onward into the darkness, already lightening a little in the east.

Dawn was breaking as they climbed their last hill and ran down toward the marshlands. A red light loomed over the greyness of the sea. The marshes themselves seemed heavy and undistinguishable - patches of land and dark creeks of salt-water running into one another. Out in the bay the foam-topped breakers came rolling sullenly in. When at last they turned through the gate, and went slowly up the rough road - marked out with white stakes - which led up to the tower, the dawn had actually come, the night was a thing of the past, although its shadow seemed to hang low over the grey land.

The sea had been lately over the rough road, and progress was difficult. At last they reached the little bank of shingle on which the tower was built, and Davidson, with a little sigh of relief, stepped wearily down. While Carter unlocked the front door and busied himself arranging a bed and lighting a fire, Davidson walked down to the edge of the sea, whose white-topped waves were dragging back the shingle as they fell and broke, with a dull grinding noise.

Never, it seemed to him, had the beauty of loneliness appealed to him more strongly than at this hour of dawn. The birds were silent, the wind had fallen, there was no sound whatever from the sleeping land. Only the eternal breaking of the waves continued - a sound which was more like the background for stillness, grim and mysterious, inevitable as existence itself. Far away now seemed that crowded court, with its eager faces, its rapt issues, - far away seemed the importance of wealth, the great question whether he should remain amongst the millionaires - the world buyers, or take his place amongst the poor men of the earth. What did it matter, after all, this kingship of the cities, with their lack of perspective, their crowded hours, their strange, artificial atmosphere? The value of these things was, grotesque, for a moment, - distorted. He had been wise to come here, he told himself, as a breath of the morning wind stole, faint and fresh, across the salt sea. Perhaps he would be wiser still if he defied fortune and stayed here always.

Carter summoned him, and he went reluctantly indoors. He ate some biscuits and drank some milk. Then, as dawn broke over the sea, a fiery red, and with many suggestions of troubled weather in its angry glow, he opened the window and threw himself upon the little iron bedstead with its lavender-scented sheets.

Chapter 42

There was one person in London who knew Davidson's whereabouts, and from him there came no word. To Davidson himself there seemed something unreal about the long hours which he spent in solitude, wandering along the sea front, following the sands left by the receding tide - himself a lonely figure on the great grey plain. A storm of rain once blew in from the sea, but mostly the day was still and colourless. To Davidson, after the long hours in the crowded courts, his directors' meetings, his self-imposed mask of ease and confidence, the relief of this absolute solitude was immeasurable. It was just the season of the year when nature and those who minister to her seem alike to sleep. It was too early for any thought of spring; the storms of autumn lay behind. A certain quietness seemed to hang over the land, as though, indeed, sea and resisting sands were exhausted with the long struggle of the winter.

Towards afternoon came some few moments of flickering sunlight. Davidson sat on a wooden bar on the top of one of the dykes, and above his head a lark was singing, a little timidly, a little doubtful, even, of his lonely music, but still lending a note of real life to the still, grey world over which he hovered. Davidson looked at the queer stone tower on its bank of shingle, and blessed the chance which had led him to purchase it. He looked inland to the little red-tiled village, to the deserted quay, from which all the fishing-boats had been dragged high and dry along the straight line of raised dyke which formed the footpath between him and the village. As he looked, he became conscious that someone had started out from the village along the dyke top. Far away at the other end he could see a slowly approaching figure. His heart gave a little beat. Was it a messenger at last, coming to bring him his fate? He looked up again to where the lark was singing. It seemed, after all, so small a thing! Nearer and nearer the figure came, near enough, at last, for Davidson to be able to distinguish something of its outline. Then he rose to his feet with a quick indrawn breath - a little cry of surprise to which there was no one to listen. For this was no messenger from the village coming. It was a girl in a long grey cloak, and a hat which she carried in her hand, as though the fresh salt air of the marshes was something also to her. Davidson saw the neatly arranged brown hair blown into confusion about her face. Against the empty background he recognized the poise of her head, the firm but delicate walk, the slender, swaying figure. He knew who it was that came, and it seemed to him that from that moment he knew, too, other things! His sense of proportions was suddenly shifted, - enlarged, perhaps, - altered certainly. He understood things which before had been mysteries to him. He understood, as though in some moment of inspiration, that riches or poverty, life, even, or death, are the incidents of life before its greatest truths. Nothing that he could think of seemed able to hold his thoughts. His heart was beating to music, the lark was singing to him a song of her own - singing in weak, tremulous notes a song of life and love and passion! He rose to his feet and went to meet her. She stopped short and faltered for a moment. He hurried on.

'Eileen!' he said

She held out her hands. Her eyebrows were upraised, her mouth was quivering, her eyes were seeking his with a sort of plaintive earnestness. 'It is true, then!' she said 'You are really here!'

'I'm really here,' he said, 'and it is really you! Nothing else seems to matter very much, - and yet, I would like to know why you alone, of all the world, should have discovered my hiding place.'

She laughed, and seemed quite unconscious of the fact that he was still holding her hands. 'I have been ill,' she said. 'I came down here to rest. Last night I heard in the village that you had arrived, that you were here alone. I knew then,' she continued softly, 'what had happened. I felt that I must come, if it was only for a few moments.'

'It was very nice of you,' he said.

Then they stood side by side in a silence charged with a sort of impotent passion. Why had she troubled to come, he wondered, now that the bubble of his wealth was burst, - she, who had held him to her cold-blooded compact, who had bound him to her by as sordid a bargain as ever the mind of woman could have conceived.

'I'm glad to see you,' he said, 'and yet I don't know why. You did not hesitate to leave me without word of you, as soon as you saw the breakers ahead.'

She drew a little away, looking at him as though she had only half understood. 'When I lost the bond by which I held you,' she said, 'I could scarcely expect you to continue to pay. I have thought it all over since, until I think that I have drunk in all the shame which a woman could feel. It was a hateful, miserable thing, but then my life has been a hateful, miserable thing ever since I was a child, and I did long, yes, I did long,' she added fervently, 'for something a little different.'

'You disappeared, then,' he said slowly, 'because you imagined, naturally enough, that so soon as you had lost your hold upon me, I'd be only too glad to free myself from our engagement?'

'Of course,' she said, the colour slowly staining her cheeks. 'There was no doubt whatever about that. Only since then I have understood how great a mistake I made. If things had turned out differently,' she continued, 'I'd never have dared to come to you, to tell you this and to ask for your forgiveness. But as it is,' she added, 'you cannot misunderstand me any longer, can you?'

'I suppose not,' he said.

'I wanted to come and tell you that I was sorry,' she continued softly, 'and to remind you that you are still young, and that the loss of a fortune is not the most terrible thing in the world. I heard yesterday that you were out upon Noble Point, close to the quicksands. You know it is never safe there, with these winter tides. Life is not a thing to be trifled with. It may seem terrible to you just now to have lost your great fortune, to be once more a poor man. These things, after all, don't count for much against the gift of life. I know it sounds like humbug to hear me talk like this, but they were gossiping about you in the village. One man was saying that he shouldn't be at all surprised to hear that you had disappeared, and to find - to find - ' she added, with a little shiver, 'your body come up the creek with the next tide. You wouldn't do anything like that, would you?'

'Not a ghost of a chance,' he said. 'Besides, I'm not quite a pauper yet.'

'You have lost the case, haven't you?' she said quickly. 'They seemed to think so in the village, and I heard that Mr. Brooke said his niece had come into a million pounds.'

'Up till last night, at any rate,' Davidson said, 'nothing was decided. The judge reserved his decision.'

'Then why did you come down here?'

He drew her a little closer to him, and looked into her eyes. 'I think, dear,' he said, 'that it was Providence which sent me.'

They walked along the sands. The sun still shone. And then, as they turned back, they saw along the dyke a boy riding a bicycle, a boy with a leather satchel around his waist, and the rim of whose bicycle was red. He pressed her arm.

'This is the messenger who brings us knowledge of our fate. In a few moments you will know whether you are to become the wife of a millionaire or a working man.'

'If you could only understand,' she said, 'how little it matters!'

'I came down here, for one reason, to escape the shock of hearing the news before others. Now I simply don't mind.

There are greater things in the world than the Letlakana Mine!'

He took the telegram from the boy, and opened it. He read it out aloud:

Counsel met in judge's private room by appointment today. Have reached compromise agreement with plaintiffs.

Davidson spun a coin to the boy, who caught it deftly, remounted his bicycle and rode away. Then, turning to Eileen, 'You see,' he said, 'you've brought me luck.'

'I only hope,' she said, as they turned together toward the tower, 'that I may bring you happiness!'

Davidson met Mrs. van Heerden a few months afterwards, and was struck at once by her altered expression. They came face to face at the corner of a street, and both involuntarily stopped.

'I hope,' Davidson said, politely, 'that you're making good use of my money.'

'And I hope,' she said, laughing, 'that you are making more fortunes from my mine.'

'I'm doing fairly well, thank you,' Davidson said, 'but you know that I have a wife to keep now.'

'And I'm married,' she said. 'I'm trying to reform Stephen.'

'I hope you're succeeding.'

'On the whole, yes!' she said, smiling. 'We live at Barnes, and he goes in to the city every day. He has bought a share in a business. We're not millionaires yet, but one never can tell.'

'At any rate,' he said pleasantly, 'looking at you, I'd say that you find it better here.'

'Don't mention the place, or anyone in it,' she said, with a shiver. 'Thank Heaven, I'll never have to go back to it! Stephen is doing very well, and half the money is still settled upon me. You have no idea,' she continued, 'how domesticity has agreed with him.'

'It's made a lot of difference to me,' Davidson said.

'I never saw you looking so well,' she said. 'Now I must hurry. I'm going to call my husband. We're going to lunch.'

'And I'm going to fetch my wife for the same reason,' Davidson said, smiling. 'The best of luck to you both!'

They parted

Davidson walked to his appointment.

THE END